SAVAGE JUSTICE

A Ryan Savage Thriller | Book 2

JACK HARDIN

First Published in the United States by The Salty Mangrove Press.

CHAPTER ONE

THE MIDDLE EASTERN night held a chill that had already started to settle into his bones. He really hated the cold. Over the last several years, he had trained in the wet jungles of Brazil, the mountainous forests of Virginia, and the sandy beaches of North Carolina. He didn't mind those. He didn't even mind the deserts—in the daytime. It was the fifty-degree loss of temperature overnight that really got to him.

But tonight wasn't part of any training exercise. This was the real deal.

He focused past the irritant of a low mercury on the thermometer and continued to pan the horizon with his night vision binoculars, alternating his gaze between the open desert to his left and the barren ridge above the cliffs to his left.

The young E-5 Delta Force operator was on overwatch on top of a neutral ridge. His pack lay on the ground in front of him. On it rested the barrel of his Heckler and Koch

416 carbine—designated the M27. The assault rifle was chambered in 5.56 NATO and had a 16.5-inch barrel. With a multi-position telescopic buttstock and proprietary gas piston system, the weapon was incredibly accurate. There was no other frontline battle rifle that compared.

Above the soldier, a hundred thousand stars twinkled against the black mantel of the desert sky. Two hundred meters downslope his troop lay asleep, tucked into their RON ("remain overnight") hide along the base of a rising cliff face.

He had already gotten his sleep for the night. But he still felt unusually tired. When his turn in the rotation came up, it had taken his Sergeant Major two full minutes to wake him. After plenty of prodding, shaking, and cursing it finally took the toe of the ranking soldier's boot in his ribs to wake him from his slumber.

That was almost two hours ago. But even now he couldn't seem to shake the weariness he felt in his eyes and the muddled haziness he was experiencing between his ears. It was like he had taken a sleeping pill and couldn't shake it off. They had just under an hour before BMNT ("Beginning of morning nautical twilight")—dawn—when they would pack up and continue on to their final waypoint. Maybe the movement would serve to wake him up.

He saw a shudder of movement in the distance and zoomed in near where his troop was sleeping. His commander, Major Dennis Archer, was out of his bag. He lay a hand against the face of the cliff and leaned over as though looking at his feet. His mouth suddenly yawed open and the E-5 watched his Major vomit up the contents of his stomach. He wiped his mouth on the back of his sleeve and then stumbled along the base of the cliff like a town drunk, his knees buckling, his head moving from side to side. He walked twenty yards into the open and started shaking his head like he was trying to rid his ears of an irritating song.

What he did next sent an eerie chill down the back of his E-5 on overwatch.

Major Archer kneeled down on the desert floor beside a rock the size of a small chair. He placed his hands on either side and, with no thought to pain or consequences began to bash his forehead on the top of the rock. *Thunk.* He did it again. *Thunk.* Again. *Thunk.*

His E-5 flinched and keyed the mic of his multiband inter/intra team radio. "Commander. *Commander.* What are you doing?"

Thunk.

His commander was not responding.

Thunk.

"Team 8, this is Crawler. *Wake the hell up!*"

Thunk.

His team was not responding. Everyone was mic'd. Out here you didn't sleep without your earpiece in. No one, however, was stirring.

Blood was pouring down the officer's face. His movements were slower now, and he started to wobble from side to side.

Another flutter of movement came from the troop's hide. The operator on overwatch turned his attention to it and watched as his Sergeant Major and the troop's ranking

NCO, Hopper Carlson, stumbled away from the three remaining operators still asleep on the ground. As if viewing a rerun the E-5 watched as his Sergeant Major struggled away from on legs that looked like they were about to give out. He leaned over, set his hands on his knees, and evacuated the contents of his stomach. He wretched for half a minute until there was nothing left to come up. Then he removed his hands from his knees and stood.

A gunshot rattled across the dark stillness of the desert.

The Major's body was sprawled across the rock, the side of his head now displaying a massive hole where the bullet had found its exit.

The E-5 had a fleeting thought that perhaps this was some kind of hazing. the first mission as a special force warrior, as a full-blown Delta Operator.

But the hopeful idea quickly faded as he recalled the nature of their mission and the prevalence of known insurgents within the general region. This was not a hazing, it was not a soldier's version of a collegiate prank. Whatever was happening out there was real. It was nightmarish and real, the scene from a hideous and distasteful horror movie.

He returned his attention to his Sergeant Major, who had moved five yards from his previous position. He was staring down toward his feet now, unmoving. leaned down and picked up a large rock in both hands. Then he started hitting himself in the face with it.

"Sergeant Major!" What in God's name was happening? "Sergeant Major Carlson!"

Thunk.

Suddenly, Carlson dropped the rock and let out a blood-curdling scream. He grabbed both his ears and shook his head before kicking at the dirt while running in a tight circle.

"Sergeant Major!"

Carlson stopped abruptly. He looked up at the stars and blinked. And before his subordinates knew what was happening he withdrew his sidearm, set it to his temple, and pressed the trigger. His head kicked to one side and his body crumbled to the ground.

The E-5's hands were trembling now. He had been trained for nearly every possible scenario on the battlefield. But he had been fully unprepared to watch his two superiors suddenly act as if they were possessed and then take their own lives. While on a mission no less. Everyone had seemed fine before they settled in for the night: jokes, quiet laughter, and easy banter.

He keyed the microphone to his satellite radio. "Eagle Base, this is Crawler 03. Come in."

He waited several seconds. "Eagle Base reads Crawler 03. Go ahead."

"Eagle we have—have a problem. Streak and Rover are down."

There was a pause. "Say again Crawler 03. Did you make enemy contact?"

"*Negative*. Streak and Rover *are dead*. They came out of their bags and—and killed themselves with their own pistols. One—one right after the other."

He knew he was speaking with Corporal Robins. The base Lieutenant Colonel would still be asleep, if not just waking.

"Standby Crawler 03."

He waited for what felt like an eternity. He used the uneasy silence to surveyed the carnage below, still unable to believe what his eyes had seen. He looked back to the hide. Still, no one stirred. These were the kind of warriors who would wake if a feather touched down within thirty years of their position. But now two gunshots had gone off in close proximity and yet they continued to sleep.

Finally, a deep voice pierced the silence—the voice of Colonel Art Dunford. "Crawler 03, this is Solo 1. Please repeat."

He recited his previous transmission, telling the officer of the odd and unsettling behavior of his Major and then his Sergeant Major before they took their own lives without a moment's hesitation.

"What is your position?"

"I'm on overwatch. Franks, Colton, and Smith are in their bags in the position relayed to base last night. I can't get them to wake. They're not responding to me."

Another long pause. "And no enemy contact? Before or after the... events."

"No, sir."

"A bird is in the air. Twenty-two minutes out. Stay on overwatch for ten and then make your way down and join your troop. Try and rouse them if you can."

"Yes, sir."

"Eagle, out."

He set the mic down and stared off into the distance. This wasn't real. It couldn't be real.

A wave of exhaustion washed over him again, causing a mild panic to well up inside. *What the hell was going on?* He suddenly remembered his gas mask, buried inside his pack. He scrambled to his knees and slid his rifle to the side. Lifting up his pack he tore through it and located the mask. He pulled it out, removed his helmet, and slipped the mask over his face, then pulled the straps taught.

There were no WMDs in Afghanistan, and he had no explanation for what was going on. But maybe local insurgents had released a toxin or nerve gas the air.

He kept his eyes downslope and scanned the horizon, trying to avoid looking at the bodies of his dead leaders as he listened to his shaky breaths echoing inside his mask.

He was no longer thinking about how cold he was.

CHAPTER TWO

Nine Months Later

MY LUNGS BURNED as my feet shot across the fifth front yard in the last thirty seconds. Up ahead, the greasy-haired man darted between two houses and disappeared from view. I pumped my legs even faster and turned after him, cutting between the houses just in time to see him scramble up a stockade fence and vault over.

On the other side, a lady screamed.

Reaching the fence I quickly scaled it and dropped into the grass of yet another backyard. I located the source of the scream. A young, slim lady was sunbathing on a lounge next to her pool. She was sitting bolt upright now and when she saw me she looked more irritated than scared.

"Sorry," I called behind me and didn't take any time to explain. I reached the gate, yanked it open, and cut across the front lawn and back onto another street. He was still a good twenty yards ahead of me, but I was finally gaining on him.

There's something about chasing down an elusive fugitive that is supremely satisfying.

I watched him reach the end of the neighborhood, cross the street, and tear across the front lawn of a preschool, quickly disappearing around the far corner of the building. Within moments he reappeared with a panicked look on his face as he decided where to go next. He locked defiant eyes with me before shooting back across the grass toward a neighboring building that I was fairly certain was a dentist's office.

The reason for his sudden change of course appeared from around the corner huffing like an asthmatic teenager. When Brad Pierce—my best friend and agency partner— saw me, he smiled and quit running.

Great, he was going to let me do all the work.

I gave him the bird as I ran by and followed Travis Harker to the next building where he was already on the far end of its mostly empty parking lot. From there he charged into a busy street filled with midday traffic speeding by.

By sheer luck, an SUV missed him by inches, and the driver slammed on his brakes and let the world know his opinion on the matter by laying on his horn for an obnoxiously long period of time.

Looking both ways I skirted a couple of cars and made it to the other side where Harker was racing down the sidewalk weaving in and out of pedestrians.

They say it's the small things in life that count. A young boy—possibly eight or nine—was stepping out of a hobby shop just as Harker risked a glance back at me. The shop's glass door swung outward and caught Harker's entire body just as he was turning around.

It wasn't pretty.

The glass shattered, sounding like a small explosion, and the top hinge tore away from the frame as it took the force of the impact. Harker was thrown to the ground amid a thousand pieces of broken safety glass.

I drew up and my feet crunched over glass as I came and stood over him. His nose was clearly broken; it lay at an unnatural angle. Blood was gushing from it and running freely onto his T-shirt.

I didn't know where the boy's parents were, but he looked down at Harker, then to the handcuffs I'd just taken out, and then back at the broken door. "Cool!" he exclaimed. "This is awesome!"

A large man appeared behind him wearing an apron and holding an unfinished model airplane. "What'd you do to my door?" he barked.

I flashed my badge and apologized, then quickly explained what had happened. "I'm sure your insurance will take care of the replacement," I said. A crowd had started to gather, so I pulled Harker to his feet and forced him into an alley a couple of storefronts down. The boy tried to follow, but I sent him away.

Once in the alley, I threw Harker back to the ground where he landed with a painful grunt. A moment later Brad appeared beside me. He leaned over and placed his hands on his knees while he tried to regain his breath.

"Hey," he said, still wheezing, "you...got him."

"You need to lie low on the doughnuts. I can't keep doing all the work."

"I redirected him! You'd still be chasing him if it wasn't for me."

"So you're an overpaid scarecrow?"

"No," he frowned. "I'm not overpaid."

Returning my attention to Harker I kneeled down, rolled him onto his stomach, and cuffed him. Harker had been on the loose for the last three months, wanted for hacking into government servers containing information on terrorists aboard.

I looked at my wristwatch and cursed. "Your little antics are going to make me late for an important party."

He coughed and tried to look up at me. "If I—I would have known that I might've made you chase me longer."

I brought my foot back and sent the toe of my shoe into his ribs. I was pretty sure I cracked a rib or two and he howled out in pain.

"Let me know if you want to keep being a smartass," I said. "There's more where that came from."

I tossed my truck keys to Brad. "Bring my truck over. I'll wait with him here."

"What? So now I'm a taxi driver?"

"Yep. An overpaid taxi driver."

CHAPTER THREE

AFTER GETTING Harker booked and locked away for the night I drove back to Key Largo, where I kept my houseboat in a permanent slip at Cozy Crawfish Marina. I boarded and took a quick shower before getting out, shaving, and then combing my black hair with the help of a little pomade. I opened my closet door and located the one suit I owned in the back, then pushed past the long row of T-shirts, polo shirts, and a hand full of button-downs before tugging the suit free.

I laid it on the bed and examined it. It was a single-breasted, two-button navy blue. I hadn't worn it in over six months. Not since my boss, Kathleen, was thrown an awards ceremony for her dedicated service to Homeland Security. My daily uniform generally entailed cargo shorts and a T-shirt; a polo shirt on days when an assignment required me to dress up. With most of my investigative work being done in and around the Florida Keys, anything more would only draw attention. Most of the time extra attention was a bad thing, so the suit never came out.

I donned a white undershirt and then a crisp white dress shirt that I'd picked up from the dry cleaners yesterday. After buttoning up the shirt, I pulled on a pair of nylon blend dress socks before slipping into the suit and donning a pair of brown Oxfords. I finished the ensemble with a bright green tie and a brown belt. Stepping up to the mirror mounted on the bullhead I adjusted the knot on my tie and decided I looked as dapper as I was going to get. After packing a small overnight bag I grabbed my truck keys from a bowl in the galley and stepped back out onto the dock.

"Well, look at you!" I turned to see Edith Wilson smiling at me from the shade of a wide-brimmed straw hat. She and her husband Rich lived on a catamaran at the other end of the marina. The two of them were like an aunt and uncle to me. At least, what I thought it might be like to have an aunt and uncle—I've never had much family to speak of. Edith was holding a leash with a Yorkshire Terrier attached at the other end. "What lucky girl have you been hiding away from us?"

"No girl, Edith. It's an old friend's retirement party."

"You look like a fancy banker, or maybe one of those models you see on the cover of GK, or GQ—I can't ever remember the name of that magazine."

"Thank you."

The dog stopped sniffing at a piling long enough to look me over and offer a shake of the tail. I walked over and scratched between his ears. "Hey, Sunny."

"Are you still on for dinner with Rich and me tomorrow night?"

"You bet I am."

"Good," she beamed. The Wilsons had two grown children that they no longer had the opportunity of seeing very often. Their daughter resided in the greater San Francisco area and was a floor manager with Google, where she often tipped the work scales at eighty or ninety hours each week. The Wilsons' son worked for an overseas construction company and currently lived in Dubai. I knew that in some small way I had come to function in their lives as a child or nephew. The sense of family went both ways. "I was thinking we could try that new Mediterranean place off Rock Harbor. How does that sound?"

"You know I'm always good for Mediterranean."

We said goodbye, and I got into my truck and tossed my overnight bag onto the seat beside me. The engine growled to life as I keyed the ignition and backed out of the space. I rolled down my windows, letting in a fresh breeze that was completely foreign to any smog-choked city and raised them again as I picked up speed and navigated onto US-1.

I connected my phone's Bluetooth to the radio and spent the next hour and a half listening to a playlist that spanned across the decades: Pearl Jam, Johnny Cash, The Righteous Brothers, and Kings of Leon. The sun was beginning to set as I worked my way into downtown Miami. Rush hour traffic had already cleared and the city's bars and restaurants were beginning to hum with a nightlife that was hard to beat anywhere else in the state.

I turned off Biscayne Boulevard and into the covered circular drive at the front of the Dominion Hotel, a five-star establishment that rose twenty-two stories above the

Magic City. I waited for the Escalade in front of me to advance before pulling up and putting the truck in park. I grabbed my bag and my phone and stepped out. I handed the keys to the valet and after he gave me my claim stub, I headed inside to check in at the front desk.

The interior was regal: white marble flooring inlaid with elegant swirls of grays and blacks, wide crystal chandeliers, and plum-colored curtains pulled back from the windows. Sharp corners and crisp lines gave the room a modern vibe. I stepped to the front of the line and waited.

"May I help you, sir?"

I approached the counter and slid my driver's license across the shiny granite. She glanced at it and worked her fingers over the keyboard. "Just the one night, then, Mr. Savage?"

"Yes."

I returned her kind smile. She had Asian features, high cheekbones, and silky black hair that lay just above her shoulders. One would have to be blind to not recognize how beautiful she was. She grabbed a blank key card, ran it through the magnetic programmer and handed it over in a small paper sleeve. "You're in room 1754. You'll need your key to access the twenty-second floor where your party is. Just scan it on the card reader inside the elevator."

I thanked her and stepped away from the counter. I waved down a concierge and, after handing him my bag and a ten-dollar bill, I recited my room number and asked him to place my bag on the bed. Then I located the bank of elevators and took one to the top floor.

As soon as the doors slid back, the sounds of cheery conversation, the tinkling of silverware on plates, and soft jazz playing over the speakers set the mood for what promised to be a memorable evening. I stepped out onto a massive open-air patio, which was hemmed in along the perimeter with glass paneling. An infinity pool glowed blue in the encroaching darkness and nearly a hundred guests were mingling with drinks in their hands. The wait staff was making their rounds with trays of hors d'oeuvres. On the north end of the roof was a covered bar with dim ambient lighting and a long wooden bar top. I made my way over and grabbed a whiskey sour before heading over to where most of the guests were assembled. Everyone was dressed for the occasion, men in suits and women in classy, fashionable dresses with their hair set in perfect fashion. A cool sea breeze blew across the roof and rustled the fronds of several potted palms. A perfect Miami night.

A man with close-cut silver hair was talking with a couple who had their backs to me. He seemed to lose interest in the conversation as soon as he spotted me and quickly excused himself. His smile grew larger and his cool gray eyes livened as he approached me. "Savage," he said, "how in the hell are you, Son?"

We shook hands and exchanged one-armed hugs as we held our drinks away from us. "I'm great. It looks like someone knows how to throw you a goodbye bash."

"That would be my daughter. Yes, she has a real knack for planning things like this."

"I was starting to think you weren't going to get a real retirement party," I said.

Lieutenant Colonel William McCleary had been my battalion commander during my time with the 503rd MP Airborne. He was not only the best commander I'd ever served under, but he was also one of the best men I'd had the privilege of knowing. McCleary kept a continual focus on his men and his mission over that of furthering his own career. Sometimes that got him into trouble when he pushed back against orders from the Pentagon that he thought were imprudent or would put his men in harm's way unnecessarily. I knew it was one of the reasons he decided to turn out into the civilian world. The further you advanced in rank, the more political things became; kissing ass and courting the favor of generals and politicians often gained priority over those under your command. McCleary had never been a man to compromise his standards on the altar of success. The Army would be slightly diminished now that he had stepped away, but I knew he would have a positive influence on whatever he put his hand to.

"The general threw me an on-base party before I left," he said, "but my daughter wanted to make sure I got to see as many people from over the years as I could."

"I'm glad she did," I said. "You've been out for, what, four months now?"

"Four months tomorrow." He wagged his finger at me. "You know, you left a gaping hole in your unit when you decided to get out. I never was able to find another officer the enlisted men respected as much as you."

I looked into my glass and swirled my whiskey. "I hated to leave. It felt like I was abandoning my family."

"Well, you weren't. You did the right thing by being there for your grandmother. There aren't too many men who would have made such an honorable decision."

"Thank you, sir."

Two years ago, when my grandmother was dying of cancer, I made the choice to leave the Army so I could take care of her. Never knowing when I might deploy again, or for how long, left me wondering if she might die while I was gone. And that was not an option. From the time I was five years old she had raised me alone, and now, in her old age, she had no one else to take care of her. I missed the hell out of the Army, especially the tight-knit brotherhood, but not once did I ever find myself regretting my decision.

"You keep that 'sir' stuff up with me and I'll deck you before the night is over," McCleary said.

"Yes, sir," I grinned.

"Have you started dating again?" he asked.

I shook my head. "It doesn't feel right yet. Too soon. Some mornings I wake up and it still feels like Michelle and I are still married. Like maybe she's gone to the grocery store and I'm just waiting for her to get back." As if I had done something to anger the gods, my wife of nine years died in a car accident just five days after my grandmother passed. Within the span of a week I'd lost the two most important people in my life.

"It will come in time, Savage. But you can't rush the process of moving on. You'll know when you're ready."

"Yeah," I said quietly. He would know. He had lost his wife to cancer three years ago. I attended her funeral and saw how it completely wrecked the colonel.

"So," he said, "you're working with Homeland now?"

"Their newest division, the Federal Intelligence Directorate."

"Anything fun?"

"Possibly," I smirked. "Rico Gallardo."

Rico Gallardo had been the most notorious counterfeiter in modern history, floating hundreds of millions of U.S. dollars around the world's economies. A few months ago, I had been sent down to Guatemala, along with the Secret Service, to take down his organization. I had been the one to send the final shots into the criminal's body, so ending his life.

"No kidding," McCleary said. "Impressive."

"So what's your next step?" I asked him. "I may have heard a rumor or two that you've started your own company."

"I have. It's a niche investigative agency. We only serve clients within the government. We're working alongside NCIS and DoD to advise on procedures and to assist in high-level or stalled investigations."

NCIS is the Naval Criminal Investigative Service, the Navy's primary law enforcement agency. To work with both them and the Department of Defense in any kind of advisory role would have taken some serious relational and political clout. With over twenty-five years of investigative experience within the military and a character of stone, McCleary was the perfect man to take on such a contract.

I said, "So you're functioning as fresh eyes from the outside?"

"Basically, yes. As you well know corruption within the Armed Services can go pretty deep. Their investigators often run into political backlash if they start nosing around in the wrong places. Since we don't have to worry about that we can charge ahead and get the right heads to roll."

McCleary was visibly enthused. He was a good man, and I was glad to see that he was able to continue doing what he loved. "I'm happy for you, sir."

He leaned in and lowered his voice. "We landed a sensitive contract from the Pentagon a couple weeks ago. If you ever want to join my team, look me up. I'd hire you in a heartbeat."

I arched an eyebrow. It was one hell of an offer. "I appreciate the vote of confidence," I said. "Right now I'm happy with my work at the FID. If something happens to change that, I'll certainly give you a call."

McCleary looked beyond me and a frown creased his brow. He extended his hand to me. "Great to see you, Savage. Look me up next time you're in Virginia. I'll take you to lunch and we can catch up a little more. These kinds of gatherings just don't lend enough time."

We shook hands. "Certainly will, sir."

"Go Hard or Go Home," he said.

I smiled at hearing the 503rd's motto. "Always."

He gave me a final nod and as he stepped past, I saw his smile fade, replaced quickly by the frown that had begun to appear before he shook my hand. I turned to see two men in suits standing near the elevator. The first man wore a custom-fitted suit with a royal blue tie. He was my height— six foot three—and looked like either a light-skinned

Italian or a dark-skinned Frenchman. His black hair had a wet look, hung loosely over his ears and stopped before it reached his shoulders. His sharp nose seemed too long for his face.

The second man was short and stockier, and his thick brown hair was wavy and uncombed. He wore an unimaginative suit that was clearly off the rack. It hung limply over him and his pant cuffs gathered loosely at his ankles. He tugged uncomfortably at his tie; a man used to camping out in an office where he didn't interface regularly with the public. Donning a suit to make an appearance at a formal party was clearly out his wheelhouse and beyond his expertise.

McCleary shook both men's hands. They followed him to an area of the rooftop where fewer guests were assembled. Once there, they stepped in close and spoke in quiet tones.

I spent the next couple of hours catching up with several buddies from my old unit, most of whom were still on active duty. We discussed their recent deployments, some of my work with the FID, and developments in the Middle East since I'd gotten out. Seeing them again reminded me just how much I missed the military, the brotherhood it offered and the bond that resulted from participating in a unified mission. I had gone to war with several of the men on this rooftop. There were a few who should have been here, fallen brothers who didn't make it back.

I finally returned to the bar and ordered another whiskey. Before I knew it, a stunning woman was at my elbow.

"Mind if I join you?" Her voice was sultry, and she had a body to match. A long blue dress clung to her shapely form and wavy blonde locks cascaded around her back and shoulders.

I answered with an indifferent shrug.

"Having a good time?" she asked.

Having a beautiful lady to make conversation with was always welcome. But I wasn't interested in being hit on tonight. Having my wife come up in conversation with McCleary had been hard enough. I wasn't in the mood for flirting.

"Look," I said, "if you were looking to go home with someone then you're barking up the wrong tree."

Her eyes narrowed on me. When she spoke again her voice was cool and measured. "I'm actually Lieutenant Colonel McCleary's daughter. And he didn't raise a floozy."

I closed my eyes, feeling the fool. I looked back at her. "I'm sorry," I said. "I didn't know—"

"Don't worry about it." She waved me off. "This is Miami. I'm sure it's easy to get the wrong impression. Get me a drink and I'll forget about it."

I motioned to the bartender. "What will you have?" I asked her.

"Vodka cranberry."

I relayed her request. "Your dad was telling me you planned all this," I said.

"Yes." She looked around at the guests and a smile formed on her lips. "We had a much larger turnout than I thought."

"A lot of people love your father. I'm one of them."

She turned back to me. Her eyes were stunning, their vibrant blue piercing even inside the low lighting. "How do you know him?"

I took a healthy sip of whiskey before replying. "He was my last commander. The best man I ever had the pleasure of working under. You're lucky to have him as a father."

"Yes," she said. "I am." She looked past the length of the bar and back outside, where her father was still standing off to the side wrapped up in a conversation with several men that I knew to still be on active duty. "The military was his life for so long. It's been nice having him around more."

"Are you working with him in his new company?"

"I am," she said. "Although it's Dad who has the quizzical mind. He's brilliant. I mostly keep the business end of things running."

"He seems to like his new line of work."

"He really does. More than I think either of us expected. The military was such a large part of his life for so long he wasn't sure how well he would manage the transition. But he's doing more fieldwork again like he was as a junior officer. It suits him."

"He was telling me he's scored a couple of solid contracts with the Defense Department."

"Yes," she smiled. "He's hit the ground running."

Someone caught her eye from across the bar and they motioned for her to come over. She grabbed her drink and extended a hand. "I don't think I caught your name."

"Savage. Ryan Savage." I shook her hand.

"Well, Ryan Savage, I'm Charlotte. It was a pleasure meeting you. Perhaps we'll meet again one day."

I watched as she moved easily across the floor in her high heels to where a party of several other ladies were mingling. One of them, a young brunette, shot me a flirtatious wave. I smiled back and then returned my attention to my drink. I finally left the bar area and walked to the edge of the roof and looked out onto the waterfront and took in the view of Biscayne Bay. The city twinkled beneath me, and out on the water yachts were moored in place, many of them hosting parties of their own.

I wasn't old by any means—just thirty-four—but I had come to realize that what really matters in life are the people you know and love. Anything can be bought with money, but the relationships are the true gold in life. Of all the parties buzzing in Miami tonight, I was proud to be at this one.

I finished my drink and, after saying goodbye to those still remaining at the party, I returned to the elevator. I couldn't find the man of the hour but did make a mental note to shoot McCleary an email later this week and wish him luck on his new career.

I took the elevator five floors down and located my room. It wasn't a waterfront view. It looked over the tower across the street and the cars and pedestrians below. But I didn't mind. I was tired. Brad had called me at 4 AM and roused me out of bed in what ended up being a very long day of locating, and then finally chasing down, Travis Harker. I could have easily driven back to Key Largo tonight, but I wanted to wake up feeling rested after sleeping in late. I slipped off my shoes, hung my suit, shirt, and tie on a hanger in the closet and then brushed my teeth before slipping in between the sheets.

I closed my eyes and soon drifted into sleep.

Until an urgent knock on my door woke me just two hours later.

CHAPTER FOUR

PSYCHOLOGISTS SAY that we dream every time we sleep, that it's just a matter of remembering them or not.

I rarely remember mine. But that night I dreamt of my wife. We were on a sailboat, just her and me, cruising over crystal blue waters and talking about where we wanted to visit next after we left Aruba. Her belly was beautifully rounded—she was pregnant. She slid next to me and had just pressed her lips to mine when I was jolted awake by a loud succession of knocks on my bedroom door.

I've always been a light sleeper. Years of overseas deployments will do that to a person. But being suddenly awakened after a romantic dream about your dead wife takes a few additional seconds to recover from.

I woke staring at the ceiling, trying to push back an enormous wave of sadness that came over me once I realized that my most recent experiences had not been in the realm of reality. Another knock at the door brought me fully back into the present. I grabbed my Glock off the nightstand

and swung my legs out of bed and onto the floor. The red digital display on the clock read 2:37 AM.

I figured some drunk had partied too late and had the wrong door. Still, with the line of work I was in I didn't have the luxury of being assuming too much. I stepped back and gripped my gun in both hands.

"Who is it?" I called out, mostly irritated that I'd been woken up.

"Ryan, it's Brad. Dude, open up."

Brad? What was he doing here?

I would know his voice among a million, but I checked through the peephole just to be sure. It was him all right: hefty frame and blonde hair trimmed in a high-and-tight, strong nose that hooked slightly to the left, piercing green eyes.

Lisa was standing behind him. The image was distorted through the small piece of glass but she looked as though she'd been crying. Lisa was a waitress at our favorite watering hole in Key Largo. Every time Brad asked her out she seemed to come up with a reason why she couldn't do it. I was somewhat surprised to see her with him.

Flipping back the latch lock I opened the door and squinted into the light of the hallway.

"What's going on?" I said. "What are you doing in Miami?" They both looked like they had just come off a date. Brad was wearing dark slacks with a blue button-down shirt; Lisa, a short green dress that clung to her like plastic wrap.

"I brought her into the city for a date tonight," he said. "Listen, I've got some bad news."

Behind him, Lisa smeared her mascara as she wiped away a tear.

"Your friend, the Colonel. Colonel McCleary. He's dead."

CHAPTER FIVE

I BLINKED HARD. "WHAT?"

Brad lowered his voice. "Can we just come in?"

I turned and walked back into my room, holding the door open behind me until I felt Brad take up the slack. I went in and sat on the edge of the bed. I was still in my boxers but failed to make the connection that a lady was present. "What do you mean, he's dead?"

"We were just coming out of the club across the street when we saw all the commotion. I finally found a police officer who would tell me what happened. I remember you saying you were staying here at the Dominion, so when you didn't answer your phone I flashed my badge at the front desk and they gave me your room number. They're saying that Colonel McCleary fell from his balcony."

I stood up and walked to the window, yanked back the curtains, and peered down into the street seventeen stories below. The street was bathed in red and blue lights, pulsating to a rhythmic frequency. A small crowd had gathered on the northern edge of the chaos, huddled against a line of crime scene tape that served to form a cautionary perimeter.

"What happened?" I said, still looking down.

"No one has reported anything unusual," Brad said. "The investigators are in his room now but from what I was told it was either an accident or suicide."

Each day, people end their own lives for a multitude of different reasons. Many times they don't show clear signals before going through with it. But I had seen the Colonel just a handful of hours ago, looked right in his eyes. What I saw were the eyes of a man enlivened about his future and the new start that his company would provide for him and his daughter. He had been full of optimism.

My career in the military had trained me to read people— McCleary himself had personally helped me to refine those skills—and I was good at reading people; their tones, inflections, and body language. There had been nothing in William McCleary that indicated he was on the brink of taking his own life.

As for an apparent accident, the idea was almost laughable. Annual deaths from guests falling from hotel balconies could be counted on one hand. Nearly all of them were drunken college students or wayward toddlers.

Behind me, Lisa was blowing her nose into a tissue. I turned around. "Let me get dressed," I said. "I'm going down there."

* * *

THE ELEVATORS OPENED, and we stepped out into the lobby. The lights from the emergency vehicles pulsed through the large panel windows facing the street. Curious guests were huddled in small groups along the marble floor. A couple of the women were blotting away tears, testaments to a well-planned night gone wrong.

A cocktail lounge was positioned in the corner past the checkout counter. The bar was closed for the night and the lights were dimmed, but the plush leather chairs and the seating along the bar remained accessible. Brad offered for Lisa to wait there until we came back, promising we'd return soon. She nodded, entered the lounge, and selected a seat. We exited out the front door into the high-ceilinged expanse of the porte-cochère and then out onto the sidewalk. Onlookers were gathered everywhere; across the street, along the sidewalks, and up against the crime scene tape. I led the way around the first group of fire trucks and police cars and stopped at the perimeter. Ten yards in front of me lay a body covered in a white sheet. It was laying in the street, just off the sidewalk. Blood from the impact had slung onto the curb.

It was all that was left of Lieutenant Colonel William McCleary.

"Do you know what floor his room was on?" I asked Brad.

"Twentieth."

I craned my neck and looked up. I finally picked out which one I thought it was. The light in the room was on, and the balcony door was open, but there was no one out there. The investigators were probably in the room. Brad followed my gaze. "Yeah, I think that's the one," he said. "This young guy was within a couple of feet of McCleary landing on him. He had just finished his shift as a bartender down the street." He nodded toward the back of an ambulance. "He was over there earlier debriefing with a badge. They must have sent him on home."

"How long ago?"

"A little before two o'clock. So, maybe forty-five minutes."

I doubted that any cameras caught what happened up on McCleary's balcony. For one, it was too high up for street levels camera to grab it. Second, there weren't many people out at two o'clock in the morning. The odds of getting any kind of cell phone footage of what happened on the balcony were pretty slim.

There was nothing else to see here. "Let's go," I said. We traced our steps back to the lobby and Brad caught Lisa's attention. He waved her over. "I guess we'll head back to Key Largo," he said to me. "What are you going to do?"

I shrugged. "Nothing I can do. This isn't my investigation."

He placed a hand on my shoulder. "I'm sorry, Ryan. I really am."

"Thanks, man." I said goodbye to him and Lisa and then returned to my room deep in thought.

When I was growing up, my grandmother had a neighbor who used to stop by and visit at regular intervals. Wallace Jones had been a decorated investigator with the LAPD for over thirty years before retiring to the rural mountains of Colorado. We lived far away from any city—the bus drive alone was nearly half an hour—and I spent the better part of my childhood roaming the foothills, wading through streams, and camping under the stars. The nearest kid to my age lived over five miles away so I learned to keep busy with shooting my .22, making traps to catch squirrels and coons, and fishing. My grandmother didn't allow for much TV time, so Wallace stopping by was often the highlight of my week.

I would sit for hours on the front porch, listening to Wallace recount case after case from the old days. My grandmother would shoot him a warning glare when his facts started to venture into gruesome territory. The gritty details, of course, were my favorite, and Wallace would usually fill me in on them when my grandmother wasn't around.

It was the old man's singular influence that developed my mind to see connections or threads that often seemed invisible to others. Had it not been for him and his stories I would have never considered becoming a military police investigator.

Now, as I lay on a hotel bed in the dark, Wallace's words came flooding back into my mind. "Go with your gut, Ryan. A good investigator will always go with his gut."

I had seen those words keep me straight and true in every case I'd ever worked. Sometimes things were cut and dry. But sometimes even the cut and dry cases seemed to be telling you a little harder, that you might find something below the surface if you just took the time to look.

And that's exactly what the small voice in the back of my mind was telling me as I stared at the red dot in the ceiling's fire alarm.

Something just didn't add up.

CHAPTER SIX

MY EYES OPENED to a shaft of sunlight coming through the curtains. I looked over at the bedside clock: 7:04. I'd last glanced at it just after 5:30. Some sleep was better than nothing. I went into the bathroom, turned on the cold water, and stepped in. My skin and muscles tingled as they imbibed the cold. I placed a hand on the tiled wall and leaned in, letting the water run across my back.

The events from early this morning didn't seem real. It all felt eerily like the week I had lost my wife; it seemed like a dream.

But it wasn't. McCleary was dead, and by my personal accounting, it wasn't an accident. He must have poked his nose a little too far into the wasp's nest. Someone wanted him dead because they wanted him quiet.

I thought of the two men who McCleary had engaged in hushed conversation at the party. One of the two looked like he had dressed for the occasion. The other seemed like he had thrown something on so he wouldn't stand out.

Like they had come to the party not to congratulate the Colonel on his retirement, but to talk shop.

I turned the water off and grabbed a towel from the rack on the wall. I stepped out, dried off, and changed into khaki shorts and a blue polo. Then I pocketed my wallet and went downstairs to get some breakfast.

The Dominion wasn't the kind of hotel that offered a complimentary continental breakfast. This was a long way from a La Quinta or Best Western. They had three different restaurants to choose from for breakfast. I hadn't been in a hotel this nice since I went to Vegas last year for a weekend of gambling with Brad.

After stepping off the elevator I entered the first restaurant I came to—The Palazzo. It looked as good as any. I approached the attendant and lifted a finger when he asked how many were in my party. I followed him farther into the restaurant and he placed me at a table near the window.

Picking up the menu I decided on the eggs Benedict and waited for my coffee. I watched as outside, a megayacht left its moorings and headed for open waters. Palm branches swayed in a gentle breeze just outside the window and the sun gleamed off the water. I wasn't the biggest fan of cities, but this view right here, I could get used to it.

Two tables over, a young blonde-haired lady blew her nose into her napkin. She was wearing jeans, a green blouse, and wraparound sunglasses. She set the napkin aside, took her fork up, and mindlessly picked at her eggs.

"Charlotte," I said, and she looked toward me. It took a couple of seconds for recognition to set into her face.

"Ryan." She leaned back in her chair and tossed her hands out. "I don't even know why I'm here. I can't eat anything."

She looked miserable sitting there alone. "You want to join me?" I asked.

She looked back to her plate, took a moment to consider, and then nodded. "Sure." She stood up and grabbed her purse, then settled into a chair across from me.

"I'm so sorry, Charlotte. I can't believe this."

"I can't either," she said softly. "Dad...he walked me to my room after the party was over. We were the last to leave. The next thing I know the cops are knocking on my door." She still had the sunglasses on and she snuck the edge of a napkin beneath the frames and blotted another tear.

A waiter appeared and placed an empty cup in front of me. He filled it with coffee from a pitcher and took my order. Charlotte said she was done with her food at the other table and instructed him to deliver her check here.

I took a sip of my coffee and set the cup down. "Have you spoken with the investigator this morning?"

"No," she said. "He told me they probably won't know anything for a couple of days. He did say they didn't see anything on the surface that indicated that something was amiss." She pursed her lips and shook her head. "He didn't kill himself, Ryan. And I can tell you this too, he wasn't drunk. He probably had four drinks over six hours. Dad was perfectly lucid when he escorted me back to my room."

"What do you think happened?"

She looked away. "I'm not sure."

"I saw two men speaking with your father last night. It didn't seem to be light-hearted party conversation." I let the inference hang.

She bit down on her bottom lip but offered nothing in response.

"Charlotte, we only spoke for a few minutes last night. What you won't know is that I'm a lead investigator with a lesser-known division within Homeland Security."

She perked up a little. "You are?"

"If what happened to your father was no accident, if he really was murdered, then I won't stop until I find out who did it, and why."

"You would do that?"

"Charlotte, your father had an enormous influence in my life, both as a man and an investigator."

She seemed to relax a little and fidgeted with a spoon resting on the table. "We just got this new case a few weeks ago," she said. "I think Dad's death might have to do with that."

"The Pentagon case?" I said.

"Yes. But how—"

"Your father mentioned it to me in passing last night. He offered me a chance to come work with him."

"That was you he asked? He spoke about you after the party was over. Just not by name."

"What is this case with the Pentagon?"

"I honestly don't know. He kept that one close to the chest. He went to Sarasota about a week ago and when he came back his entire disposition had changed. It was nice to see him finally lighten up at the party last night. Our secretary booked his travel but he wouldn't say what he was doing in Sarasota. Now I'm thinking it was to protect me."

"Those two men he was speaking with, do you know them?"

"No," she said. "I put the guest list together and emailed out all the invitations. I don't know who they were."

Charlotte's phone rang from inside her purse. She took it out, glanced at the screen, and answered the call. "Hello?" I watched her lips tightened into a fine line. Over the next minute, she listened as the caller did all the speaking. "Thank you. I'll be there soon." She hung up and then removed her sunglasses and wiped at her eyes. They were red and puffy, the clear result of a night spent grieving over a horrible tragedy. "I'm sorry," she said. "I know I'm a mess."

"You don't need to apologize to me," I said.

"That was the detective. No witnesses have come forward claiming to have seen anything. There was nothing in his hotel room that testified to a break-in and nothing to indicate a skirmish. They want me to come down to the station to answer a few more questions." She grabbed her wallet, unzipped it, and withdrew a couple of bills. She placed them on the table. "Please make sure the waiter gets this."

"I will." I stood as she returned her sunglasses to her face and stepped away from the table. I extended my hand, but she surprised me by stepping up to me and giving me a hug. I wrapped my arms around her shoulders. "You'll get through this," I promised.

She stepped back. "Thank you, Ryan. I'd better go."

I watched her walk across the restaurant and turn out toward the lobby. When my food arrived, I found that I wasn't all that hungry either. I had a couple of bites and a second cup of coffee before I started feeling restless and decided to leave.

It was after nine o'clock when I checked out of my room and the valet brought my truck around. I shot a glance down the street as I pulled out. The immediate area where McCleary's body had landed was still cordoned off and a police officer stood by to keep curious passersby continuing on their way. My heart was heavy as I took the Dolphin Expressway across the city and turned south, where I finally joined up with US-1. I still couldn't believe that my former commander was dead. That his daughter and my instincts failed to see it as an accident didn't help matters. I wanted to stick around and start asking questions. But it was too early for that. At the very least I needed to wait and see what the detective came up with before starting up an investigation of my own.

I was listening to Tom Petty sing "Runnin' Down a Dream" when he was interrupted by my phone ringing. It was my boss, calling on a Saturday. She typically kept long hours that often included working weekends. I answered the call, and it connected through my truck's Bluetooth.

"Hey, Kathleen. How's your vacation going?"

"When I get one, I'll let you know. How far are you from the office?"

"I've just left Miami. A little more than an hour?"

"I hate to ruin any plans you may have had, but I need you to come in. Pronto."

"Okay. I'll come straight there. Want to clue me in?"

"Not over the phone."

She hung up, and I glanced at a passing speed limit sign before nudging the accelerator a little closer to the floor.

CHAPTER SEVEN

THE FID OFFICES were located on the south end of Key Largo, perched along the Gulf and looking out over Sunset Cove. The two-story building sat in the center of a vibrant green lawn hedged in by royal palms.

I scanned my badge at the front gate and drove my truck into the parking lot. I parked facing the water, and in the distance I saw a couple boats cruising over the calm water, the water spreading out behind them.

I stepped out of the truck and was greeted by a gentle breeze coming off the water. Above me palm fronds whispered and lulled lazily through the air. I strolled to the employee entrance at the side of the building, scanned my badge, and stepped into the air-conditioned lobby. The first floor of the building was for support staff, crime lab, and IT. On the north end was a small weapons armory containing assault rifles, body armor, flashbang grenades, night-vision goggles, and the like. I said hello to the security guard who seemed to be concerned with a game he was playing on his phone.

Kathleen calling me in on a Saturday prompted me to take the stairs two at a time. I opened the stairwell door and stepped out onto a carpeted floor dotted with desks, cubicles, and floor-to-ceiling windows that served to lighten the entire space. Kathleen's corner office was at the other end of the floor and I made my way to it. As far as I could tell she was the only one up here. I often got work done on a Saturday, especially if an investigation was coming to a head, but it was usually fieldwork. Other than a quick stop to check out a couple of assault rifles and some body armor, I couldn't remember the last time I'd come into the office on a weekend.

I rapped lightly on her open door and stepped in.

"Ryan," she said. "Thanks for coming in. Have a seat."

Kathleen Rose was two years over fifty. She kept her graying brown hair a dark chestnut and trimmed to just above her shoulders. She was slim, of average height, and I was pretty sure that today was the first time I'd seen her when she wasn't wearing a business suit. Instead, she wore black jeans and a blue collared blouse. Dressed down but incredibly classy.

Kathleen had recently come over to Homeland from the CIA. She was hardly out of college when the CIA sent her to Romania as an undercover operative at the tail end of the Cold War. In the thirty years since she had and spent three years as Brussell's Chief of Station. Her interest in switching agencies and coming to Homeland was prickled by incessant politics at Langley and a personal desire to move to southern Florida to be near her sister. She was a top-rate professional and even though we butted heads from time to time, she commanded my full respect.

"I hope I'm not interrupting any weekend plans," she said.

"I was planning on power washing the houseboat. Nothing that can't wait."

She swiveled in her chair and grabbed a piece of paper off the printer. She slid it into a blue folder, shut it, and laid it on her desk.

"Okay," she said, "I'll get right to it. I got a call this morning from an old colleague who now works in D.C. He's been a squeaky wheel about some concerning things he's noticed within the Department of Defence." She handed the file across her desk.

I took it and flipped it open.

She must have noticed the atypical blank look on my face. "Is something wrong?"

"No." I blinked. "No—I'm not sure."

"The most confident agent I've ever had working for me is stumped and looks a little shell-shocked. Want to explain?"

My eyes raked over the remainder of the papers in the file before coming to rest again on the image staring up at me.

It was a photo of William McCleary.

CHAPTER EIGHT

"Ryan?"

I looked back up. "I'm sorry. What's this about?"

"William McCleary. Retired Army Colonel. He died last night."

"I know."

"You know?"

"He was my former Battalion Commander."

Kathleen's face pinched into a frown. "You knew him?"

"That's why I was in Miami. I was at his retirement party last night."

She shook her head. "You would think that with all the intelligence resources we had around here that I would have made the connection." She studied me for a moment. "I'm sorry, Ryan."

"Thanks." I tapped the file. "Why am I holding a file on him?"

"I suppose you know that he started an investigative firm that only does contract work for the government."

"Yes."

She leaned back in her chair. "Ryan, what do you think happened last night?"

I sighed. "I'm not sure. There are whispers of suicide or an accident. An accident?—no. And suicide...not a chance."

"So you think he was murdered?"

"My gut says so. But I don't have any facts to conclude that."

"Well, if it makes you feel any better, I think your gut is right. And I'm not the only one. Tina Cox is the Miami PD investigator assigned to McCleary's death. As of an hour ago, she was instructed to conclude that McCleary's death was an accident. She'll continue with her investigation and see what she can turn up. But in a few days, she'll write up her report to that tune and close it out."

"Instructed?"

"We don't want to raise suspicion that anyone thinks there was foul play. He fell by accident, nothing more to say. It will look as if no one is the wiser and we're all moving on. If Cox does find anything, like CCTV footage, or a witness saw something then she'll forward that our way. However, I have a contact at the Pentagon who called me first thing this morning. He's one of the few people, if not the only one who has any idea about what's going on. He's the individual who got McCleary involved in a case that he thinks led to his death."

"What kind of case?" I asked.

"He won't tell me. Not over the phone. Now that McCleary is dead my contact is pretty skittish and frankly, doesn't know who to trust."

"Why did he come to you?"

"For starters, because he trusts me. His name is Douglas Peterson. He worked with me at Langley for several years before moving over to Defense. And second, he came to me because the FID has such a low key presence within the intelligence community. Peterson is one of the directors of technologies at DARPA. He has an office in the Pentagon."

DARPA was the acronym for the Defense Advanced Research Projects Agency. DARPA was an arm of the Defense Department, responsible for the development of emerging technologies for use by the military. On one level it seemed like a bunch of nerds playing with a three billion dollar annual budget that allowed them to keep building science fair projects. The agency made headlines a few years ago when it revealed a new project called 'Warrior Skin', an exosuit intended to alleviate musculoskeletal stress on soldiers while carrying heavy loads. Other notable projects included a computer-derived rifle scope that combined various features into one optic, an autonomous robotic satellite-servicing project, and extensive research into various forms of cancer.

"Did he give any clues at all about what he gave to McCleary?"

She shook her head. "He's terrified right now, and rightly so, if your former colonel's death wasn't an accident. He trusts me and he'll talk with whoever I put in front of him. So I'm sending you to D.C. to meet with him. He's tossed his personal cell and is using a burner phone right now. You'll find his number in the file."

"When do I leave?"

"I know you just came from there, but your plane leaves out of Miami in just under four hours."

"No private jet this time?" I asked.

"I need you as inconspicuous as possible. The last thing I want is for some mole on the inside of the intelligence community to check charters flying into D.C. You're flying coach into Baltimore, then renting a car for the drive into D.C. Hotel arrangements are in the file. Speaking of which, when you're done reviewing them, the files stay here at the office."

"Okay. Are you putting Brad on this with me?"

"You're working this one solo. The fewer people involved, the better. Besides, I need someone to locate that source in the Criswell case. If you get down the road on this and need his help, let me know. In the meantime, keep me updated. I'll have my phone on me all weekend."

I stood up and headed for her office door.

"Ryan." I stopped and turned back. "Be careful."

CHAPTER NINE

I MADE my way to my desk and looked out the sprawling window in front of me. My view was enviable: a sheet of water stretched all the way to the horizon, spotted only by the occasional mangrove island. I scooted my chair in and opened the file.

McCleary's boutique agency was Pursuant Services. He had filed the business name with the state of Maryland five months ago, formed an LLC a week after that, and retired from the service two months after that. Pursuant had been operational since then, with an office in D.C. just off DuPont Circle.

A quick online search showed no public information on the company, which wasn't unusual being that McCleary didn't cater to the wider public. With his network of connections and his contract with the DoD, he must have hit the ground running.

The million-dollar question was, what had he been investigating when he died? He had obviously gotten too close to the truth, whatever that might be, and it seemed likely that he had been silenced for it.

Besides his daughter Charlotte, McCleary had a secretary and one other investigator on the payroll, a Travis Barlow. According to the file, Barlow was also ex-military, a retired Army Major who had spent much of his time as an enlisted soldier in the role of Military Special Agent with the Army Criminal Investigation Division Command (ACIDC). A little further digging showed that McCleary and Barlow had met while on temporary duty (TDY) in Europe over ten years ago.

I decided to wait and reach out to Barlow when I got to D.C., after first speaking with Peterson. It seemed that Peterson was the horse's mouth, and I wanted a clear picture of what was going on before I questioned anyone else.

I grabbed up my desk phone and dialed the number for Peterson listed in the file. It rang, kept ringing, and never went to voicemail. I tried a second time with no luck. I decided to call again before I left for Baltimore.

I closed the file and stood up, then slipped it into my center desk drawer before returning to the stairwell and exiting the building.

* * *

I DROVE BACK to my marina and returned to my house-boat, where I hung up my suit, returned my Oxfords to the bottom of the closet, and emptied my overnight bag before stuffing it again with fresh clothes. I left the toiletries in the side pocket. My service pistol was in the truck, locked in the console, and I brought a hard-sided carry case so I could check it on the airplane. I locked up, stepped off the boat, and walked down to the Wilsons' catamaran. Neither Rich nor Edith were there. I stood at the end of the dock and called their phone. I left a voicemail, letting them know that I was leaving town unexpectedly on business and wouldn't be able to make dinner tonight. I returned to my truck and checked the time. I still had a couple of hours to burn before starting the return trip to Miami so I decided to head over to my favorite watering hole, the Wayward Reef.

Five minutes later my Ram's tires were crunching over the crushed shells of the bar's parking lot. I turned off the truck and stepped out. It was after noon and the sun was high and blinding in the sky. The two plastic dolphins mounted on The Reef's eave smiled down at me as I stepped inside.

It was lunchtime on Saturday, and the place was buzzing with happy conversation and easy laughter. The wide roller door at the back was up, allowing a welcoming breeze to come inside, stirring the various accoutrements hanging from the ceiling and walls: fishing lines drooped between the exposed rafters with clothespins clipped over them, grabbing onto iconic vinyl record covers from past decades that seemed to know what good music was really all about, stuffed fish replicas, and a shrimping net that hung loosely from the ceiling. I loved living in the Keys, and The Reef and the good people who frequented it was just one of the many reasons why.

I made my way to the bar where a muscular man with growing love handles was perched on a stool. I slapped him on the back as I bellied up to the bar. "You get any sleep last night?" I asked.

"Hey," Brad said, "I was just about to step outside and call you." He shook his head in response to my question. "I dropped Lisa off at her house and then went home. But no sleep. Not after all that. You okay?"

I shrugged. "I guess." I wasn't. With each passing hour, I could feel a wave of deep-seated anger growing steadily inside me.

The swivel door leading back into the kitchen swung out and a round man with red, glowing cheeks stepped out. He had a snowy white beard and hawkish eyes that seemed to never miss a thing. "Ryan," he said, and then reached out and shook my hand. "I'm sorry about your friend. Brad was telling me about it."

"Thanks, Roscoe." Roscoe was The Reef's owner and a good friend. He grabbed a tall glass, filled it full of beer from the tap, and set it in front of me. "That one's on me. Now if you'll excuse me I've got to make a phone call back in the office. I was expecting a delivery this morning, but it still hasn't shown up yet. Let's make sure we talk later."

"Sure thing. And thank you." I took a long draw off the beer. I was about to set the glass down when I decided to drain some more. The refreshing liquid felt good going down. Just what I needed. I don't drink while on the job, but since I still had some time before the flight, and I wasn't scheduled to land in Maryland for another five hours, I had no second thoughts at getting after this one.

I felt a light hand on my back and turned to see Roscoe's granddaughter standing behind me. Amy's blonde hair was shot through with bright pink highlights, and she had a smile that could brighten anyone's cloudy day. She was carrying a food tray, and a waitress apron was strung around her waist. She reached in and gave me a hug from the side, saying how sorry she about what happened in Miami.

"Do you want something to eat?" she asked.

"No. The drink is fine for now. Thank you."

She went around to the front of the bar and set the tray down. "Lisa called me this morning. She's not doing so well after seeing all that last night."

"I feel really bad about it," Brad said. "Of all the gin joints in all the world I had to take her to one right down the street from the scene."

"You didn't know," Amy said. "It sounds like she had a great time before that."

Brad winced and brought a hand to his chest. "You okay?" I asked.

"Yeah," he grunted. "Fine. Just feel like someone is stabbing me at random times of the day."

"It's probably just gas," I said, and he shot me a chastening glare. He hated it when I said that.

Three months ago, Amy's boyfriend had gotten involved with a bad group of criminals who were running illegal cargo up into the Bahamas and through the Keys. The whole affair didn't end up working out well for him, and in the course of our investigation, Brad had been shot twice in the chest at point-blank range. By some miracle, the former Marine hadn't died. His recovery was slow, and he had only returned to work a couple of weeks ago. He still got sharp pains in his chest every so often. The doctor said they were nothing to worry about, that they were part of the healing process.

"I think maybe I shouldn't have tried to chase down Harker," Brad said.

"If I remember correctly, I'm the one who did most of the chasing."

"But not all of it."

I leaned across the counter and smiled coyly at Amy. "You wouldn't happen to have a quarter, would you?"

She rolled her eyes and feigned irritation. "I swear, every time you or Brad come in I leave with about five dollars left in tips."

I gave her the same reply I did every time she brought that up. "I don't carry—"

"I know," she interrupted. "You don't carry change. Here." She dug around in her apron and produced two quarters. "There's an extra one. Because Lord knows you'll ask again."

I smiled at her. "Thanks, Amy."

I turned around and went to the back wall where the jukebox was sitting. The thing was a gem and the most recent addition to The Reef. Vintage vinyl albums sat in rows beneath the glass and were moved by a robotic arm once you made your song choice. The exterior was framed in salvaged wood from an old pirate ship and the keypad's buttons were shaped like tiny anchors. I leaned over and scanned the playlist. There were a hundred and eighty songs to choose from. I was about to select Guns N' Roses' "Welcome to the Jungle" when my eyes fell on a title I hadn't played before: "All Along the Watchtower". I remembered that Colonel McCleary had enjoyed listening to Hendrix. I located the playlist number, slipped a quarter in the machine, and selected the song.

As the drums kicked off and Jimi's electric guitar quickly joined in, I found myself remembering the Colonel, the kind of man he was, the dedicated leader, father, and friend. The song was halfway over before I returned to the bar with my mind freshly steeled to a promise to uncover the truth.

I finished my beer as Brad made conversation with someone beside him. After a few minutes, he turned back to me. "Any more news on what happened?"

I pushed my empty glass to the side and nodded toward the back deck. He got off his stool and followed me outside, across the deck, and down the narrow dock where a few fishing boats and skiffs were tied off.

Now that we were alone, I wasn't worried about being overheard. I filled Brad in on my meeting with Kathleen and what little was known so far: how McCleary had been working on a case that was somehow connected to the Defense Department, and how that the man who had fed him the investigation was running scared, convinced that the Colonel had been murdered because he was getting a little too close to the truth.

"Any idea what McCleary knew?" Brad asked.

"No. Kathleen's contact is too paranoid to say anything over the phone. Can't say that I blame him."

"What's the next step?"

"I'm flying to Maryland in a couple of hours. Kathleen wants me to go meet with this guy and get the scoop."

Brad frowned. "Weird. She didn't mention anything to me about it."

"She's keeping you on the Criswell case. Said she wanted her best agent on this one."

"Which is exactly why I should be on it," he quipped. We started walking back and entered the welcoming shade of a cluster of palms. "But really, I'm glad it's you who gets to look into it. Colonel McCleary deserves justice."

"Thanks, man. He does."

"Just don't screw it up. I don't want to have to come in and clean up your mess."

CHAPTER TEN

THE CABIN PRESSURE started to change a few minutes before the flight attendant announced that we were now entering our descent into Baltimore and would we please set our tray tables up and ensure that our seat belts were fastened.

I looked out the cabin window and watched as the ground started to draw nearer. Cars driving along the eastern seaboard came into view, appearing first as small as ants, and then, as we continued our descent, like the modern modes of transportation that they were.

The plane banked and entered its spot in the rotation to land. It was nearing 7 PM local time. I was tired. I hadn't slept on the flight. I'd tried, but rest wouldn't come; my mind was struggling to relax with the death that lay behind me and the investigation that lay before.

There was a delay on the tarmac and we had to wait an extra thirty minutes to arrive at our gate. I deplaned, followed the terminal to baggage claim, and after another fifteen minutes of waiting at the claims counter, turned in my ticket voucher and repossessed my firearm. Kathleen had reserved a midsize sedan for me. The Hertz attendant informed me that all they currently had was an Acura TLX. Not being one to complain about an upgrade, I signed the paperwork and exited the terminal. I walked across the street and found the car in the lot, then started the air conditioning before taking out my phone.

I had programmed Douglas Peterson's phone number into my contacts. If he was using a burner phone, then I suspected that the number wouldn't be valid for very long. But I think it was Einstein who said never memorize anything you could look up. That didn't always apply when working a federal investigation, but it did in this instance. I had tried to call Peterson another three times before boarding the plane in Miami. He hadn't answered. I tapped the phone number and set my phone to my ear.

It rang and then continued: five, eight, ten... *fifteen.*

I was starting to get a little irritated. I hung up and called again. It was a perfectly natural response for Peterson to be scared. I understood only wanting to talk in person and the desire to switch to a phone you could easily dispose of at any moment. But that phone didn't do you any good if you never picked it up. Unless, I started to wonder, something had happened to him, too. My concerns were alleviated when the ringing stopped and the call was answered.

"Hello." The voice was gruff.

"Mr. Peterson?"

"Who is this?"

"Your friend in Key Largo asked me to meet with you. She thought you might like the gelato from the vendor on Waterside Drive."

My response to him had been dictated by instructions in the file Kathleen had given to me earlier in the day. It was all a little silly, but I respected the effort. The man was simply doing the best he could to stay safe and out of harm's way.

"What color is my friend's hair?"

The question sounded impromptu, as though he hadn't planned on asking it. But he was still operating out of his paranoia.

"Brown. It's colored. If you need me to be more specific, it's a chestnut brown. Her words, not mine."

That seemed to settle him. "Look," he said. "I don't know how to do this. If they took out McCleary, it won't be long before they try and come after me. If they're not already."

"Let's meet," I said. "I came up here to help you. Whoever might be after you, we'll stop them."

I heard a bout of nervous laughter from the other end of the call. "These aren't the kind of people you can just stop. You think you can just fly out here, have a chat with me at a coffee house or something and—presto!—it's all better now?"

Coffee did sound really good. "No. That's not what I think. Where do you want to meet?"

"Where are you?"

"I've just landed in Baltimore. I'm in the rental car about to start driving toward D.C."

"We'll meet in Virginia. Call me after you've crossed the Potomac." He hung up.

I set my phone on the passenger seat and pulled out of the Hertz's parking area. I worked my way out of Thurgood Marshall International Airport and joined the Baltimore-Washington Highway where I began the one-hour drive southwest to D.C.

I punched on the radio and scanned the channels for ten minutes until, finding no music I particularly liked, I just gave up and turned it off.

The sun was starting to set in the west, casting an orange glow across the road ahead and stretching shadows like black taffy. I sat in silence and maintained the speed limit, recalling the last time I had been in the nation's capital.

It was three years ago, and my wife and I had come for a quick weekend visit. We spent the first day working our way down the National Mall and stopped at the Korean War Memorial. A grandfather whom Michelle never had the chance to meet had died in the conflict all those years ago.

Our second day there we slept in, ordered room service, and spent the morning in bed together. We went to lunch at the Municipal Fish Market and then caught a Nationals game at Nationals Park. It was the last weekend we had away together. Not long after I left the Army, and not long after that, Michelle was gone from my life forever, taken by a man running a red light because he was too busy texting.

I shook the memories from my mind and punched the radio again. I didn't care what crap might be playing anymore. I just wanted to forget. The memories stirred up a pain that I didn't have the luxury of sitting in right now.

The few miles I'd moved away from the city must have cleared up a rural station. Tom Petty came through the car's speakers, and I rolled down my windows and I sang along to It's Good to be King.

CHAPTER ELEVEN

An hour later I turned off Route 295 and merged onto Interstate 695, where I crossed over the Anacostia River and drove parallel to the National Mall on my right. I caught a glimpse of the Capitol dome and then the bright white obelisk that was the Washington Monument. I loved D.C., if for nothing else than for what it represented: the seat of a government that was of the people and by the people, a republic that was a beacon of freedom for so many around the world. I loved the city for what it was supposed to stand for: the ideals of liberty and the reminders of the weighty costs that were paid to maintain it. The Constitution and the Declaration of Independence reside here, and the Vietnam, WW2, and Korean War memorials stood a sobering testament to the reality that freedom is not free.

I passed L'Enfant Plaza and Benjamin Banneker Park before getting to Rochambeau Memorial Bridge and crossing over the Potomac. I picked up my phone and dialed Peterson again.

"Where are you?" he asked by way of greeting.

"Just crossed the river. Where am I going?" It was silent for several moments. I started wondering if Peterson was having second thoughts. "Where am I going?" I repeated. On my right, the Pentagon rolled by.

"Potomac Falls Park. Call me when you get here. And make sure you're not followed."

I drove for two more exits and then got off the highway, took a right at the light, and drove beneath the overpass. I slowed as I neared the park, keeping my speed under the marked ten-miles-per-hour, and followed the edge of the park until I spotted an empty parking lot. I pulled into a space and shut the car off. I called Peterson again.

"I'm here. Where do I go?"

"I'm at the north end of the gardens."

I removed my Glock from its travel case and stepped out of the car, then tucked the weapon into the rear seam of my jeans. Only the faintest glow of blue and orange brushed along the western edge of the sky. It would be full dark in ten minutes. Dim lamplight covered the bricked sidewalk as I passed beneath the low-hanging branches of crepe myrtles and worked my way toward what I assumed were the gardens. My feet left the sidewalk and echoed softly along a boardwalk sitting above the wetlands that lay on the edge of the Potomac. Reaching the end I saw a darkened figure leaning against the wooden railing. Somewhere a frog croaked. "That's close enough."

I stopped. "Douglas Peterson?"

"Yes."

"What's your name?" he asked. His voice was shaky.

"Ryan Savage."

It was quiet for a long time. "I don't know what to do. They killed William McCleary."

"Who did?"

I couldn't see his face and he seemed to be assessing me. "Follow me," he finally said.

I followed him off the boardwalk and onto a well-defined dirt path, where a bench sat beneath a maple tree. He sat and I joined him on the bench. A lamppost spilled light from five yards away and I could make out the contours of his face as the tree's leaves danced over us.

Douglas Peterson was of average height and slim build. His dark hair was cropped short but appeared to be thinning out on top. He wore dark slacks, a dress button-down shirt, and dark circles resided beneath his eyes. His features looked tired and gaunt, his skin sallow, like he had not been afforded the luxury of much sleep in recent days.

"It might be best if I started at the beginning," he said quietly. "I work for a relatively unknown agency within the DoD, the Defense Advanced Research Projects Agency. Have you heard of it?"

"DARPA," I said. "Yes, I have."

"And what do you know about it?"

"You guys are one of the DoD's research arms."

"Yes. We've created technologies intended on reinforcing the country's defense. I was behind one of those, an IR laser that can temporarily incapacitate an enemy's nerve function. In fact, that's the project I was managing when all this started." He stopped speaking and craned his neck as he looked up and then down the path. "I'm sorry," he said. "This is just getting to be too much." He leaned back and his knee bounced nervously up and down. "A year ago we had a research scientist who was working on a biologic treatment that could help astronauts with vertigo and re-entry fatigue. It was a pretty straightforward and unassuming project. Except that this scientist, rather than sending his research through the proper DARPA channels for testing and approval, gained a back door patent." He looked over at me in the dim lamplight. "So I went to my superior with it and he said he'd look into it. Three months later I never heard anything else. So I went back to him and followed up. He said that the information was in the proper hands and thanked me for my concern.

"Now, I'm not a cop. I'm not an investigator. Sometimes I can't even find the right sock in the laundry pile. And that's why I reached out to McCleary. We were college roommates for a semester but, as you can probably see, West Point wasn't for me. But he and I kept up over the years. When I learned that he was working for the DoD as a contracted investigator, I brought this to him. After waking up to a text telling me he was dead, the only person I could think of taking this to was Kathleen."

"Do you know what Colonel McCleary might have found?"

"He and I had lunch across the river last week. He didn't have much at the time, but he said it looked like our scientist—Dr. Parker—had sent his research to MercoKline."

My brows went up. MercoKline was a multi-billion dollar pharmaceutical company. "So Dr. Parker sold his research off to big pharma?"

"I think that's exactly what happened. And three days ago I really started to get nervous. I was working late and stepped out to get something to eat from the cafeteria downstairs. When I got back, there was a note on my desk. It looked like it was created in a standard word processing program. Printed on standard paper. All it said was 'You and your friend need to stop looking into Dr. Parker's work. If not, there will be consequences to your actions.'"

"Do you still have it?" I asked.

"Are you kidding me?" he scoffed. "Whoever these people are, they're not amateurs. I work in the Pentagon for crying out loud. You don't just walk right in there and put a note on someone's desk. You have to have clearances for that kind of thing. Whoever made that note wasn't going to be stupid enough to leave prints on it. Besides, who was I going to take it to?"

"Do you think Dr. Parker may have left the note? Or your boss?"

"My boss was in Bali celebrating his wedding anniversary. And Parker's gone. He left a few months ago and went to work for MercoKline."

Somehow that last bit of information didn't surprise me. "The Colonel had a partner at Pursuant," I said.

"Yeah. Travis Barlow. I don't think he's privy to any of this. It's my understanding that he's somewhere over in Asia working a case with NCIS. McCleary was the only dog on this trail."

"What about his daughter, Charlotte? She worked with him." I thought about my conversation with Charlotte at breakfast this morning, how she seemed to think that her father's death was no accident either. I wondered just what she might know.

"She had a mid-level role," Peterson said. "I don't know what he may have told her because I don't know what he may have uncovered this past week. I think she was mostly interfacing with DoD's contract acquisition department and also assisted with case research. Their secretary did all the billing, travel booking, and accounting."

I went on to describe the two men I'd seen on the hotel rooftop last night; the well-dressed European man and the frumpy white man. For all I knew, they had been the ones to get rid of the Colonel. "It didn't seem to me that they were friends there to celebrate his retirement," I said. "If I had to guess, they were talking shop."

Peterson shook his head. "I don't think I know them." He leaned forward, placed his head in his hands, and sighed.

I thought through everything he had said: the crooked scientist and his transition over to MercoKline, of his direct report lacking the proper motivation to look into it, and the note placed on his desk by someone from the inside. But even though I was now armed with this information, I wasn't sure where to go with it. I had a dead friend, possibly a corrupt scientist, and a government employee who was scared for his life. Not much to go on.

"Douglas," I said. "Can you think of anything else? I want to get to the bottom of this, but I'm not sure that I know how to proceed from here."

He tensed and sat up. "Yeah—I completely blanked." He started patting his pants pockets and then stood up and moved his hands to his rear pockets. "I had a… a flash drive for you. But I think I left it in my car." He looked toward me again. "I'm sorry. It's been a hell of a day. I'm not thinking straight."

"Where's your car?"

"It's in a space on the other side of the park."

"I stood up. Let's go get it."

I fell in beside him as we walked down the trail opposite the direction I'd come in. Peterson left the bricked path, and we cut through a copse of trees before coming out onto a narrow field with a soccer goal at either end and a playground perched in the center. "I'm sorry for being so paranoid," he said. "I've known something's been going on for a while now. But that note, it scared me. And with McCleary being—"

He didn't get to finish his sentence. I recognized the distinct zip of a bullet cutting through the air just as it made contact with Peterson's chest.

CHAPTER TWELVE

THE FORCE of the impact flung Peterson backward, and he collapsed on the grass. A second round whizzed by just inches from my face, and then another as the shooter tried to make good his aim once again. I yanked out my Glock and dropped to my stomach, then rolled behind the limited cover of a thick pine tree.

Between my overseas deployments with the Army and the two years I'd been with the FID, I'd been shot at dozens of times.

It wasn't something you got used to.

My heart was racing, my adrenaline pumping overtime as my autonomic nervous system did everything it could to ensure that I stayed alive.

Another round punched into the tree trunk, making me flinch involuntarily.

The other side of the field was hemmed with trees and tall grass—a black curtain of darkness that provided adequate cover for an active sniper. I was a sitting duck, with no safe means of retreating and no way of going forward. The limited cover of the pine was my only hope, but that wouldn't be the case for very long if the shooter repositioned himself and altered his angle.

I glanced toward Peterson and studied him for a moment. He lay on his back. His chest wasn't moving. He wasn't breathing. Another bullet hit higher on the tree and pieces of bark flew out into the grass. I flattened out on the ground.

The rifle was operating with a suppressor. Instead of a report echoing loudly across the park and the surrounding areas, the only sound produced by the weapon was a soft "click," like a young boy was playing with a BB gun. I guessed the distance to be forty or fifty yards, and with no way of pinpointing his position, returning fire would be pointless and would only expose me unnecessarily.

I turned my focus to the end of the field and the direction that Peterson had been heading when he was shot. At the end of the field was the north end of the road I'd driven in on. There the road swept around and disappeared. I could just see the roofs of an adjacent apartment complex about a hundred yards away, nearer to the highway. That's where Peterson must have parked.

Another bullet chewed into the ground two yards to my right. That's when it occurred to me. The sniper was no expert. He'd hit Peterson when he was walking at a steady pace in an unvaried direction. But he'd missed me after I responded to Peterson getting shot. He missed twice in fact, and now, a third time. And at no more than fifty yards away, the shot was a piece of cake, even for an amateur.

I decided to take my chances and play against the shooter's apparent lack of skill and work my way back into the cover of the gardens. Slowly, I started to crawl backward while continuing to hug the ground, trying to keep the trunk of the tree between me and the person who was trying to kill me. I knew that the farther away I moved from the tree, the easier it would be to sight me; with every foot I retreated, the less cover the tree would afford. I swiveled on my stomach until my feet were facing the field and then advanced a few more feet before digging my toes into the earth, setting my palms into the grass, and shooting forward as if I was on fire. A bullet tore past less than an inch from my neck. My adrenaline was in overdrive and it took me three seconds to reach the cover of the gardens where I continued farther in until I was sure that the trees and the vines and bushes were thick enough to hide my movement from night vision.

My feet sloshed into miry grass and I finally found the boardwalk I'd met Peterson on earlier. I reached up and climbed over the railing, then quickly retraced the way I had come in. I was at the other end of the field now, where the path crossed the road, and I paused and held behind the cover of an oak. If I stepped out, I would be in range of the shooter until I crossed and made it several yards down the bricked path. But I had no idea how tenacious he —assuming it was a he—might be in his attempts to take me out, too. Or if he even knew who I was. Obviously, my complicity with Peterson was warrant enough to want me out of the picture.

Across the field, I heard the long grass whisper and then the muted sound of a twig snap. He was on the move. A few moments later a dark shadow stepped out of the brush and into the mowed grassy shoulder of the road. He wore all black clothing, and a black baseball cap was set low over his eyes. His right hand was clutching a rifle. He moved away from me at a hurried pace and followed the road toward the apartment complex.

My gun was still in my grip. Now would be the only chance I had to catch him and start getting some answers. Leaving the cover of the tree, I stepped into the road and started running after him, pumping my legs as fast as I could. Trees, grass, and the open field flew by me as I gained on him, only to watch him disappear around a bend in the road. Moments later I saw the red reflection of a car's brake lights on the road, followed immediately by the sound of a vehicle's engine turning on. I came around the corner just in time to see a mid-sized sedan accelerating down the street. I stopped, raised my gun, and applied pressure to the trigger, but the car swung around the next bend and out of sight before I could get a shot off. I kicked at a small rock in the road and cursed into the night sky.

He'd gotten away, and I had let him.

I turned around and ran back to where Peterson had fallen. I kneeled down beside him and set two fingers against his neck to check for a pulse. He was dead. I sighed and rubbed at my brow, wondering what in the hell was going on. Two people were dead in less than twenty-four hours, and for what?

I reached into Peterson's pocket and found his keys. I stood up and looked down on him, wishing I'd had a sheet or a jacket to drape over him. "I'm sorry, Douglas." I turned and ran across the field, then back down the street until I came to the apartment buildings. I dind't know where he had parked, but I figured the most logical place would be the apartment complex. I hadn't seen any other cars at the parked when I arrived earlier.

The entrance was gated, but a pedestrian gate was set off to the left. I tugged on it and it opened to me. I walked through and fingered Peterson's key fob, and I heard a welcoming beep in response. I passed up a couple of stairwells and turned the corner. I pressed the key fob again. The five spaces down the parking lights of a white Jeep Cherokee flashed twice. I opened the driver's side door and got in.

I checked the console, the glove box, above the visors, behind the seats and under the seats. I tore apart the truck, lifted the seats, and for good measure, even lifted the hood and searched the engine compartment with the flashlight on my phone.

There was no flash drive in the vehicle.

In his frenzied state, Peterson must have left it at his office.

Frustrated, I secured the Jeep and returned to my car. As I pulled away from the park, I called Kathleen.

She answered in her typical clipped manner. "Ryan."

"Peterson's dead."

Silence for several seconds, and then, "How?"

I explained how I had met her former associate at the park and what information he had offered during our brief chat. I told her about the former DARPA scientist, his connection to MercoKline, and the warning note that had been left on his desk only a few nights ago. I told her how Peterson had been executed on our way back to his vehicle, and that the shooter had tried to take me out as well.

"Are you all right?" she asked.

"Fine. I'm heading to the hotel. I need some time to think about where to go from here. I don't know what was on that data stick, and without it, I'm long on questions and short on answers."

"Peterson was a good man," she said quietly.

"Yeah. So was McCleary. I need you to get someone over there to deal with Peterson's body ASAP. I really don't want a local resident to come across him during a nightly stroll." I gave her the rough location where the shooter had set up. "Have them check the area for casings."

"I'm on it."

We hung up as I navigated back to the highway and drove back over the river, all the while thinking of what to do next.

CHAPTER THIRTEEN

CHARLOTTE McCLEARY INSERTED the key into the lock of the front door and turned it. When the deadbolt clicked back she removed the key, opened the door, and stepped inside. She flipped on the lights.

The Pursuant offices were on New Hampshire Avenue, on the slice of road that connected DuPont Circle to Washington Circle, in a street-level suite. To the right was Swaziland's diplomatic embassy; on the left, a satellite office for a regional investment banking firm. The suite was of modest size—just under eighteen hundred square feet; they hadn't needed more than that. The extra space was intended for the addition of personnel as the businesses expanded and took on more contracts.

Charlotte's father had given her free rein to decorate the office to her tastes. His time in the military had truncated any sense of style he might have had to begin with, and she wanted to ensure that the space looked the part. The office didn't see much pedestrian traffic, but in their line of work, where professional connections and political savvy meant everything, it served to reinforce their image as leaders with a niche focus.

She had selected an industrial chic design with an exposed ceiling, metal and glass partitions, and furniture with sharp angles and bright colors set against muted walls. The concrete floor was stained a reddish-brown—English Red —with a clear layer of epoxy that served to give it an elegant shine.

Charlotte passed up the receptionist's desk and proceeded to her desk at the back. She was tired, dog tired, and wished she could have returned much earlier. The detective in Miami had asked her to remain in the city for the remainder of the day, in the event that there were additional questions. Charlotte's plane had touched down at Dulles an hour ago. After waiting for her bags, locating her car in the parking garage, and driving the thirty miles to the office, it was now an hour before midnight.

Her neck ached from the flight, and she hadn't eaten a thing since pecking at her breakfast in the hotel restaurant this morning. She set her purse on her desk, pulled out her chair, and sat down.

Her eyes found her father's desk across the room and she broke into tears again. She cried freely for several minutes, still feeling like she was in a nightmare that she couldn't crawl out of. He should be at that desk Monday morning, where he would sometimes look over at her and toss her a wink.

Charlotte gathered herself and grabbed a pack of tissues from a desk drawer. She blew her nose and dried her eyes before opening her MacBook and turning it on. She typed in her password and navigated to her email host. She had no idea what she was looking for, but she wasn't going to just sit around and wait for something to surface. Her father's death had something to do with a case he was working with Pursuant. She was sure of it. Over the last ten days, he'd become narrowly focused on a case, one that he had decided to work on his own. He hadn't shared any of the details with her. That in itself was highly unusual; he always shared information about cases with her, often asking her opinion or seeing if she could help him with a missing piece.

But lately, with each passing day, Charlotte could see the stress building in his eyes and his face and in the tense way that he carried himself. That was why she had been so glad to see him finally relax at the party last night. He had a few drinks, caught up with old friends, and, save for the two unexpected visitors who had stolen his lightheartedness for twenty minutes, seemed to forget about work for a little while.

Charlotte stood up and started walking back to the front desk to retrieve a file. She froze as her veins turned to ice.

Standing in front of her, not fifteen feet away, was a man. His right hand held a suppressed handgun. It was trained directly on her. Her entire body tensed and her pupils dilated as she stared at him. He was wearing all black; long-sleeved shirt, jeans, and a nondescript baseball cap. He was clean-shaven and had bright blue eyes and a strong jawline. He was almost handsome. She surprised herself when she spoke. Her voice wasn't shaky or wavering, her words coming out cool and collected. "What do you want?"

His expression didn't change. There was no smile, and he didn't smirk. "Your father's laptop. Where is it?"

It took a few moments for his words to register. Her eyes remained fixated on the gun, and she swallowed hard. "I don't know."

"I need it."

"It must have been in his hotel room. The Miami police probably have it."

"It wasn't. And they don't."

Her eyes flared with anger and moved from the gun to his face. "You killed my father?"

"Where do you think the laptop is?"

"I asked you a question," she said icily.

"And I asked *you* a question. Since I'm the one with the gun, you might want to answer it."

"Why?" she asked. "What did my father do that deserved him being killed?"

He shrugged. "I honestly don't know. The answer to that is outside the scope of my interests."

"I don't know where it is." Her voice was trembling now. "*Please*. I don't know anything."

He looked around the room with a casual disinterest that made Charlotte understand that she was going to die here, in this office, and on the same day as her father. Her concealed carry, a Ruger SP101, was behind her, completely useless as it sat in her purse on the desk. The dozens, if not hundreds, of hours spent at shooting ranges with her father were all for naught. When the moment finally came, she was without any means of defending herself.

The man's cold and calculating eyes came to rest on her once again. A smile finally came. It was just as she thought it would be: indifferent with a hint of play. "I'll give you one more chance. I need your father's laptop. If you don't know where it is then perhaps you can give me a possible location."

Her bottom lip started trembling. "He was a good man."

"That's not the answer I was hoping for. I'm sorry to have to do this. You really are very beautiful."

He took a step forward, raised the weapon, and Charlotte's body jerked as two shots rang out.

CHAPTER FOURTEEN

MY GUN BUCKED in my hand and I watched as the man who had murdered Douglas Peterson collapsed onto the stained concrete floor. I locked eyes with Charlotte McCleary. Her arms and hands were shaking. She was holding her breath and looked as if she were about to scream. Her eyes roved over me, but she failed at recognition.

"Please," she choked out. "Please, I—"

"Charlotte. It's me, Ryan Savage. We had breakfast together this morning."

Her eyes finally made the connection. "Ryan? God, what —who—"

I held my hands up. "You're safe now. You're safe, okay? He's not going to hurt you."

"Oh, God. He was going to kill me. What is happening?"

"I don't know." The man's gun had clattered away near a baseboard when he fell. Still, I used caution when pulling back on his shoulder and rolling him onto his back. His lips were covered in fresh blood. His eyes looked distant, but he was still breathing. Keeping my gun trained on him, I squatted down. "Why were you going to kill her?"

"He kept asking me where my father's laptop was," Charlotte said from behind me. "That's the only thing he seemed to want. And I think he's the one who killed Dad."

"Is that right?" I growled. "Did you kill my friend? Did you kill her father?"

He tried to speak. As his lips trembled, a thin rivulet of blood ran out of his mouth and down the side of his face. His chest shook, and he gave a stunted cough. He was choking on his own blood. I moved behind him and lifted him up. When he coughed again, I knew my efforts at getting him to speak were fruitless. Blood sprayed from his mouth and painted the floor. His breathing slowed and he tried to suck in another breath, gagged, and then finally went limp. He was dead.

I retrieved his gun. It was a Sig Saur P226 with custom chrome plating and a textured blue polymer grip. I stuck it in the back waistband of my jeans and searched his pockets. All I came up with was a large key ring with an attached Acura key fob, a couple of pink keys, and a purple leather strap with the phrase "I heart Taylor Swift." Nice, I thought. He had stolen the car.

"I thought... I thought it was his gun that went off," Charlotte said from behind me. I stood up. Her hands were still shaking, and I thought she might faint.

"Here." I grabbed her desk chair and slid it over. "Sit down."

She did as instructed and swallowed hard. "How did you get in?" she asked.

"Same way he did," I said. "I was driving by when I saw you inside and then saw him stepping in. Hold on." I took out my phone and dialed Kathleen again.

"Yes?"

"So, I've got another body."

"The man who killed Peterson?"

I appreciated her confidence in me. "Yes. He came to McCleary's office. His daughter was here, and he was about to get her too. I need you to keep Metro police off this. Someone was bound to have heard the shots."

"The team is about done at the park. I'll send them over to Pursuant. Maybe twenty minutes?"

"Ten would be better. I'll call you later." I hung up and headed for the front door, locked it, and came back to Charlotte. I took her hand and helped her back to her feet. "Come on, we need to go."

"Okay…" Her eyes were still fixated on the body, and it seemed like she had hardly heard me.

I raised my hand in front of her face and snapped my fingers. That did the trick. "I know this is a lot for you, but we've *got* to go, Charlotte. Is there anything you need to bring?" I repeated.

"Yes." She went back to her desk, slung her purse over a shoulder, and grabbed her laptop.

"What about your keys?" I asked. They were still on the desk, lying on a short stack of papers.

"Oh. Yes." She snatched them up with shaking hands.

"Come on." She followed me to the back door. I unlocked it and led her outside. We headed north down the alley. "Where's your car?"

"At the end of the alley. On the side street."

"Do you need anything out of it?"

She hesitated. "Maybe. Ryan, I don't know what to do… where to go—"

"We'll get to that. Do you need anything out of your car? You won't be able to come back to it."

"My suitcase. That's all."

Her vehicle was an Infiniti QX70 SUV. She pressed a button on her key fob, and the rear hatch lifted away. I grabbed her hardshell suitcase from the back and stepped back. The hatch shut and she locked the car, setting the alarm as she followed me around the corner of the building and back to New Hampshire Avenue, where my rental was parked curbside.

Directly in front of it was the dark sedan that I had watched drive away after Peterson was murdered.

I tossed Charlotte's suitcase in the back seat and helped Charlotte into the front. "Give me a second," I said. I shut the door and stepped to the other car. It was a black Lexus GS. I opened the trunk and the interior light illuminated a wood stock 30.06 rifle with an attached suppressor. A canvas pouch held five full metal jacket cartridges. I saw no accessories, only a can of tennis balls and a woman's tennis racquet.

I searched the inside of the vehicle and came up with nothing that tied itself to the man who had stolen it. Not even a phone. When my team arrived, they would take prints off the car, but I knew they would only find prints that matched a Taylor-Swift-loving, tennis-playing woman and her friends. I locked the Acura and set the keys along the back ridge of the front tire. After taking a picture of the license plate, I texted it to Kathleen and then got in the Acura. Charlotte was already buckled. I started the car and pulled out into the empty street where I whipped a U-turn and headed northeast. I entered Dupont Circle and turned out at Connecticut Avenue.

I had a better idea of why I wasn't dead yet. The assassin had killed Peterson without the assistance of night vision, a scope, or a bi-pod. It explained why he had missed me several times.

I wanted to know who sent him.

Charlotte was calmer now. "Do you have somewhere else you can go for the night?" I asked. "Someplace safe?"

"No. Not that I can think of. I just moved down here from New York a couple of months ago. I don't know anyone here well enough to call them up at midnight and ask if I can crash at their place." She frowned. "Back at the office, you said you had been driving by. Why? What are you even doing in D.C.?"

I was about to answer when a glance in the rearview mirror told me we were being followed.

CHAPTER FIFTEEN

"WHAT IS IT?" Charlotte asked. She was observing me stare in the mirror at the car behind us. It was hanging a good fifty yards back.

"We've got a tail."

She groaned and turned in her seat so she could look out the back window. "How do you know?" she asked.

"He shot out of a cross street a minute ago. When I passed that last intersection, the light was turning yellow. He gunned through the red light and slowed again. Now he's maintaining his distance. Hold on, I'm going to try something."

We were going north on 16th Street: two lanes on either side of the double yellow stripe. High-end apartment complexes and mid-range condos rolled by, each building accommodating three or four floors. The area was mostly deserted this time of night, with only the occasional vehicle turning on or rolling past. I checked the road ahead and, seeing that it was empty, pinned the accelerator to the floor. The Acura responded immediately, the speedometer moving from forty to fifty, and then to seventy within just a couple of seconds. The force of the acceleration forced us back into our seats, and I let off the gas when the speedometer crossed eighty. The engine's RPMs came down and I looked back. The car was now over a quarter mile behind us, but it had responded with a burst of speed of its own. It was coming on quickly.

I hit the brakes and spun the wheel, crossing hand over hand as the car whipped into a hard right turn. Charlotte screamed and gripped her seat with one hand and the side of the door with the other. "What are you doing?" she cried.

"They aren't trying to just follow us, Charlotte." I straightened the car and punched the gas; we flew by a park on our right and another apartment complex on our left. "If they were, they wouldn't have made their presence so obvious. They're either really bad at tailing a car or they plan on killing us. And after the night I've had, I don't think it's the former." Behind us, the car made the turn and escalated toward us.

I flipped a left onto Georgia Avenue and we tore down it, passing more lofts and old buildings that had recently experienced the benefits of gentrification. The car shot out of the side street and continued to give chase. I leaned forward, reached around, and plucked my gun from behind my back. I set it in my lap and gripped the wheel tightly in my hand. I was about to give the engine a little more gas when a pickup truck appeared from a side alley and moved into the street ahead of us without even bothering to check for traffic. He wove back and forth between lanes like he was drunk; I couldn't even pass him.

"Slow down," Charlotte yelled. "Slow down!"

I mashed the brakes, the anti-lock system engaging as I put all my weight into the pedal. The seat belt dug into my neck and my chest as the Acura trimmed the kinetic energy still hurling toward the truck at sixty, fifty, and then thirty-miles-per-hour. The truck swerved slowly into the other lane, and we missed swapping paint by mere inches. It ambled across the two left lanes and entered an alley on the other side of the road, seemingly oblivious to the danger he had just put himself in.

The episode had allowed the other car to close the distance on us. He was directly behind us now. His high beams were on, blinding me as they reflected off my mirrors. Up ahead the light at the intersection switched to yellow, and I gunned the car forward just as the driver behind me moved out and started to come up on my left. We passed under the light just as it turned red. I grabbed my gun off my lap and gripped it hard.

"Oh, God," Charlotte whimpered.

"It's all right," I said calmly.

The car pulled alongside me and drew close. It looked like an Audi, but I couldn't be sure. Its windows were blackened with tint and I couldn't see through them. The car's window came down, and I hit the brakes again, bleeding off speed and preparing to spin the wheel into a U-turn. But the driver was apparently prepared for the move. His brake lights lit up, and before I knew it he was beside me again and a bright flash came from inside the Audi. A bullet shattered my window and continued through the car, barely missing Charlotte before exiting the vehicle.

Charlotte screamed and put her hands over her ears. "Get down!" I yelled. She leaned forward and tucked her head between her knees. The driver fired off another two shots, both of them missing, one whizzing just past my forehead.

My turn.

I edged up a little closer, brought my gun up and fired off three rounds in quick succession. The first hit the door, but the next two tore through the window. The car cut a hard left and as we continued down the street, I turned and watched as it slammed into a telephone pole. I tapped the brakes and spun the car around. Charlotte screamed again and pressed her hands into the dash as the Acura's back tires skidded over the pavement. I moved into a parallel parking space on the edge of the road and jumped out of the car. "Stay here," I said.

"But what—"

"Stay here," I repeated, with a little more force. I watched the Audi as I worked my way toward it, clutching my gun in a double-handed grip. The car was at the far corner of an intersection. The driver's door was open and the right blinker was pulsing on and off. I could see steam rising from the engine and heard hissing from beneath the crinkled hood. The pole he had crashed into was in front of a print shop. This entire section of the district looked like it catered to commercial business. I'd left Charlotte parked near the side entrance of a warehouse, and across the street was a fenced-in parking lot full of old semi-trucks. No one seemed to be around to notice the accident, or the gunshots for that matter, and the road was absent of any oncoming vehicles.

I approached the car cautiously swinging around wide to the left so I could get a clear view of the inside from the open driver's side door. It was empty. I wrapped my hand around the back door handle and stepped back as I trained my gun inside. Empty too.

There was a small pool of blood on the driver's seat and a thin trail of it leading toward the print shop before disappearing altogether. I edged closer to the small standalone building and turned the corner, keeping my gun out in front and taking note of every shadow and hint of movement. The back area of the building turned into a grassy slope that led down to a dark treeline. I circled back around to the front of the building and checked the other side. He was gone. I sighed and kicked a Coke can off the sidewalk, frustrated that I let yet another door of inquiry slam shut in my face.

I could circle around the trees and see if I could pick out the Audi's driver somewhere on the other side, but I wasn't going to risk him doubling back and grabbing Charlotte, or worse.

I did a quick sweep of the Audi's interior with no luck there either. The registration in the glove box showed that it was registered to a Heidi Collins and, while I couldn't be sure that the driver wasn't a woman, I thought it was a fair bet that this car had been stolen too. Whoever these people were they clearly weren't interested in leaving a trail.

I jogged back across the street and got into the car. Charlotte's face was pale. "Did you find him?"

"No." I turned back out into the road, turned around, and headed north. "No one was following us when we left your office," I said. A mile later we pulled beneath the bright glare of an overhead light in a grocery store parking lot. "Let me have your phone."

"My phone? Why?" She reached down and dug it out of her purse. "Here."

I pulled off the case and flipped it over, examining both it and the phone. "They knew when you were at the office and they magically found us again after we left." I pressed the case back onto the phone and popped the trunk. "We need to search your suitcase."

I opened the back door and pulled her suitcase from the back seat. She followed me out of the car and met me at the open trunk. "I'm going to dump everything. I need you to search behind your clothing labels and along the seams. I'll check the suitcase. Your shoes, too."

"What am I looking for?"

"Anything out of the ordinary. A hard bump, what feels like a foreign object. It won't be large."

I unzipped the suitcase and upturned it, shaking the contents out before setting it down on the pavement and using the overhead light to search by. I traced my fingers along the inside of the zipper then searched a mesh pocket and the edge of the partition. Finding nothing, I grabbed my phone and searched the liner. "Anything?" I asked over my shoulder.

"No. Wish I knew what I was looking for."

I stopped when my palm ran over a slight bump on the inside edge. Looking more closely, I noticed a small tear in the fabric of the lining. I pinched at it and it tore back, revealing a tiny metal square less than half the size of my pinky nail. I plucked it off the plastic and held it up to the light. It was a solid piece of metal with the density of a magnet.

"What is it?" Charlotte asked.

"A tracker. And not one you can buy on Amazon, either."

"It was inside my suitcase?

"Inside the lining." I stood up.

She groaned over my shoulder. "Dammit."

I laid the tracker on the asphalt, brought out my gun, and smacked the butt against it a couple of times. The tracker crinkled, but I didn't know if what I had done was enough to deactivate it. So I picked it up and tossed it a few spaces down the parking lot.

"That means they were in my room," she said, "Unless they got into my suitcase at the airport."

"Airports have a lot of cameras along the luggage route," I said. "I'm betting on the hotel. They got to your father there."

She wrapped her arms around herself. "Can we go now? I think I'd like to just get into bed."

I zipped up the suitcase and left it next to the concrete base of the light pole.

"You're leaving it?" she asked.

"I doubt they put a second one in there, but I'm not taking any chances. Come on. Let's get going."

CHAPTER SIXTEEN

I TOOK a circuitous route out of D.C. and into Maryland. We passed through Silver Spring and I took Route 410 west into Bethesda, all the while checking my mirrors to ensure we were still in the clear. Satisfied, I pulled into a gas station and parked into a space at the front. "Wait here," I said. "I'll be right back. You want anything?"

"Water might be nice. Thank you."

I went in and withdrew two hundred dollars in cash from the ATM and handed the attendant at the counter a ten for two bottles of water. He counted my change back to me and I returned to the car. "Thanks," Charlotte said when I handed her the water. She unscrewed the plastic cap and chugged half of it down. I pulled out and drove a couple of miles before seeing a sign for the Old Glory Motel off the side of the road. I turned in and told Charlotte to wait in the car while I went inside. The small lobby was encased in dark wood-paneled walls and black carpet, on which years of foot traffic had worn a lighter-colored path that led to the front counter. I heard the distant whine of an old TV coming from the back and the flickering glow from what sounded like a baseball game. An old man with thinning lips and squinty eyes came through the doorway. He was hunched over and using a cane to maneuver across the floor.

"Evening," he said. "You need a room?"

"I do. One in the back if you've got one available. And two beds," I added.

He ran his finger down an open ledger and mumbled to himself. "I've got room 182 available. We don't offer breakfast and you have to be checked out by ten."

"That's fine. How much?"

"Seventy-two dollars. That includes tax."

That was a little steep for a place like this, but everything was more expensive in this part of the country. I wasn't in the mood to haggle. I tugged four twenties from my wallet and handed them over.

"All right," the old man mumbled to himself. "Let me get your change." He opened a drawer and counted out my change. "Here you go." I pocketed it and he gave me an old-style key with a hard plastic tab with the room number on it. "Just drive around where we are now and you'll see the room out near the corner. Park, anywhere you like."

I thanked him and returned to the car. Charlotte was quiet as I drove around the building and parked in front of room 182. Here we were out of view of the street and I was confident enough that we weren't being tracked anymore. I went to the room and opened the door, flicked on the light.

Two beds sat on the left wall with a nightstand in the middle. There was a plush lounge chair by the window, as well as a dresser and a narrow desk standing along the wall leading to the bathroom. A flat-screen TV was mounted above them. The room smelled like new carpet and the lingering scent of pine left behind by the cleaning products used in the bathroom. I'd seen far better, but I'd also seen worse. It wasn't a roach motel, but it wasn't a Holiday Inn Express, either.

I returned to the car. Charlotte was already out and standing beside it. It was a mess. My window was blown out and tiny fragments of glass littered my seat and the console. Her window, while not shattered, featured two clear holes where the bullets had punched through, small spidery cracks running away from them. I opened the trunk, and she picked through some of her belongings and gathered them into her arms while I brushed away some of the glass with my hand. When I heard the trunk close, I grabbed the assassin's gun and slid it into my bag, shut the trunk, and followed her inside, where she dumped her clothes into a dresser drawer. I locked the door, tossed my bag on the other bed, and pressed myself into the lounge chair. She sat on the edge of the bed farthest from the window and laid back into the mattress. "I can't believe all this," she said, staring at the ceiling. "This time yesterday we were just wrapping up the party. Now I'm hiding away in some crummy hotel room because the people who probably murdered my father are after me too. And I have no idea why." She let out a tired and weary sigh. "You never did say why you were at my office tonight."

I'd already been pondering how much to tell her. She'd been through enough already. "I came up here to meet a contact about your father's case. The man who gave it to your father to begin with."

"How did that come about? At breakfast this morning you seemed to know nothing about it."

"My boss is friends with the contact—Douglas Peterson. That name ring a bell?"

"No."

"He reached out to my boss this morning. After he heard about your father's death, he got more scared than he already was. Apparently, the list of people he felt he could trust was pretty short. My boss sent me up here to meet with Peterson to see what I could learn."

"That call you made tonight, back at the office, you said something about a body. Did they get to him too?"

I'd forgotten about that phone call, that Charlotte may have overheard my conversation with Kathleen. "Yes," I said reluctantly. "Driving by your office wasn't really planned. It was just off the route to the hotel I was planning on staying at. I thought I'd drive by and get the lay of the land, as it were. I saw a man in dark clothing slip in through your front door."

"I don't think I locked it," Charlotte said. "God, how could I have been so stupid?"

"You couldn't have known," I said. "What were you doing there so late?"

"I wanted to feel like I was doing something." She tossed her hands up and let them fall back to the mattress. "I have no idea what Dad was looking into. Did that Peterson guy give you anything?"

"No, not really." I only had a bare stretch of the details and didn't want to concern Charlotte with even more questions to which I had no answers.

"I wish I knew where Dad's laptop was. I guess whatever is on there is worth killing me over, too."

"Yeah," I said. "Why don't you call the detective first thing in the morning and see if they have it in evidence? They may have bagged it when they went through his hotel room."

"Okay."

The truth was, I highly doubted that Miami PD had the computer. McCleary was pushed off his hotel room balcony, which meant the killer had access to his room, which meant that they would have grabbed it after the murder had it been there. Whatever the case, calling the detective in Miami would give Charlotte something to do in the morning; she wouldn't have to go to sleep feeling completely helpless.

She sat up and came to her feet. "I think I'm going to take a shower," she said and opened the dresser drawer. She selected a few items and grabbed a towel from the rack above the sink, then went into the bathroom and shut the door. I heard the water turn on and the curtain slide shut.

I slipped off my shoes and laid my Glock on top of the nightstand, then changed into a pair of shorts and swapped out my socks for a clean pair. I could feel the adrenaline starting to wear off and it left my eyes and muscles heavy.

The shower knobs squeaked in the bathroom and I heard the water turn off. A couple of minutes later Charlotte reappeared wearing a set of silk pajamas: light blue shorts and a matching spaghetti strap top. Her hair was wet and limp and she toweled it off and slung it back. She looked amazing.

After running the towel over her head a final time, she tossed it on the floor and grabbed a hairbrush from the counter. She stood in front of the mirror and started brushing her hair out. The reality of why we were here together and that fact that she was my former commander's daughter kept the rising temperature of my blood in check. He couldn't protect her now, and by some twist of fate, I had been selected to take his place.

"Ryan?" She stopped her brush and looked at me in the mirror's reflection.

"Yeah?"

"I didn't thank you for saving my life tonight. I'm sorry we're not here under better circumstances, or in a nicer room." Her tone was as suggestive as her words and I swallowed hard, struggling to keep myself in line. I wasn't the kind of guy to take advantage of a scared and grieving woman.

"Yeah," was all I replied.

When she was done at the sink, she pulled back the covers on her bed and slipped beneath them. I brushed my teeth and turned off the lights, I got into my bed and tried to settle my mind as it raced through the day's events.

Her voice finally broke the silence. "Who do you think is behind all this?"

"I don't know. I really don't know. But I sure as hell am going to find out."

Her next words were hardly a whisper. "I can't believe he's gone."

"Get some sleep," I said. "Chances are we've got another long day tomorrow."

CHAPTER SEVENTEEN

THE MORNING CAME QUICKLY, with a couple of kids running past our room waking me just after eight o'clock. I typically get up with the sun, but I obviously needed the rest. I'd slept like a rock and woke up with both my mind and body refreshed. I left the relative comfort of my bed and stepped into a cold shower, letting the icy water roll down my neck and back as I contemplated the day ahead.

I was in the rare position of not knowing where to turn. Peterson had provided the bare bones, but someone was highly motivated to keep us from discovering what was really going on, and that made me think that the truth was far worse than we could think. I knew that a drug or medicine had been developed by a scientist working for the federal government. I knew that the scientist had probably made a deal that would allow him to profit handsomely from his discoveries and had taken the recipe and the patent to one of the largest pharmaceutical companies in the United States. But that didn't explain what that drug was or who all the people might be who stood to profit from it.

I felt like a blind dog trying to uncover a scent while still chained up in the backyard.

Even so, I had a plan.

I turned off the water, toweled off, and got dressed. When I opened the bathroom door, Charlotte was already dressed and had removed her belongings from the dresser to a plastic bag branded with the motel's logo.

"Morning," she said. "How'd you sleep?"

"Well, thanks. You?"

She shrugged. "I've had better. What are we doing this morning?"

"I want to go back to Pursuant and see if I can turn up anything. Your dad had to have left some kind of bread crumbs, somewhere." I brushed my teeth, combed my hair, and after grabbing my gun off the nightstand and my bag off the lounge chair, we took our leave of the room. I drove us around to the front and turned in the key to the front desk. When I returned to the car, Charlotte was just ending a phone call.

"That was the detective in Miami," Charlotte said. "Tina Cox. She said they don't have Dad's laptop. She also said they don't have anything else to share with me *at this time*." The way she formed the last few words served to show her discontent.

I remembered what Kathleen had said about Detective Cox, how Cox had been ordered to continue with a quick but thorough investigation, before publicly announcing that there was no indication of foul play and ruling it an accident. I hadn't received an email or phone call from Cox yet and could only conclude that, as yet, she really hadn't found anything that could help me.

I pulled away from the motel and back into the main street. "What do you want for breakfast?" I asked.

"I'm not all that hungry. But I could definitely go for some coffee." Her phone was lying in her lap. It rang and she snatched it up. "Hello?" She listened to the caller speak for half a minute. "Hold on," she said and then put the call on speaker. "Please continue. I've got you on speakerphone. I want someone else to hear this too."

The voice on the other end was laced with a French accent. "Ah, Miss Charlotte, I would prefer that only you have this information directly. It is of... a very sensitive nature."

"I'm with a man who was good friends with my father, Ryan Savage. He was friends with my father and saved my life last night. Twice, in fact."

I cringed when she said my name. I had no idea who she was speaking with or what he wanted.

"Saved your life?" the man said.

"I went to the office as soon as I got back into town last night. A man came in with a gun and asked me where Dad's laptop was. He almost killed me. Had Ryan not showed up, he would have."

"Charlotte, I am so sorry. You said twice? He saved your life twice?"

"Another man chased us down in the car. But...you said you have Dad's laptop?"

My ears perked. The light ahead turned red, and I slowed the car to a stop.

"Yes. He gave it to me the night of the party."

"How did you know him?" she asked.

"He called me the day before and said he would be coming to Miami for a party. He asked me to meet him at the hotel so he could give me his laptop."

Charlotte looked over at me. The light turned green, and I gave the car some gas. "Why?" she said into the phone.

"He hired me to examine some information on it. The files were encrypted and could not be properly transferred to an external drive."

"Hired you? What is it that you do?"

"I would prefer not to say over the phone. Can we meet? My office is in Miami. I'm sorry. I would have called before you returned to D.C., but we just finished analyzing the information on his computer."

Charlotte looked to me, unsure of how to answer. "You'll have to forgive me if we're a little skeptical," I said. "And I didn't get your name."

"I am Jacques Tissot. I am the president of GRM, an independent research lab."

"How do we know you didn't just steal the laptop?"

"Of course. Mr. McCleary called me the day he died. We texted several times as well. I can take some screenshots of the texts and send them to you if you like."

"Please," I said. "And send your address, too."

"Yes. I will do that as soon as we hang up."

"Jacques," I said. "I'm a federal agent with Homeland Security. I'm going to inform my team that we're coming to meet with you. Should anything happen to us while we're there, or soon after, you'll be a prime suspect."

There was silence for a few seconds. "I do understand. Please know that we had nothing to do with Mr. McCleary's death. I think everything will begin to make sense for you after we speak."

"I'll have Charlotte let you know when we arrive back in Miami today and provide you with an ETA to your offices."

"Very good."

Charlotte hung up. "What do you think they're researching?"

"If I had to guess, I'd say it was whatever information Douglas Peterson gave your father."

I stopped at a McDonald's and Charlotte went inside and ordered us breakfast while I called Kathleen, filling her in on the conversation with Jacques Tissot. "So tell me I'm not flying coach back to Miami," I finished.

"Get to Washington Executive Airport," she said. "I'll have a plane there for you in half an hour. And Ryan?"

"Yes?"

"I'm going to put Brad on this with you. I don't want any more dead bodies. Maybe if the two of you team up, you can get this wrapped up faster. He's down in Key West right now, but connect with him on it when you're down in Miami."

The passenger door opened just as I hung up and Charlotte got in clutching a paper bag full of food. "I thought you said you weren't hungry?" I said. "You could feed a small squad with all that."

She gave me a sheepish smile. "I tend to buy stuff when I'm nervous." She plucked a breakfast biscuit from the bag and handed it to me, then placed a cup of coffee in my cup holder. "Oh, Jacques sent over the texts he had with Dad. Here." She held the phone out to me.

I scrolled through them. They were a typical text string between two men looking to do business. It seemed like they had already spoken over the phone prior to messaging. The context was vague, not easy to understand for anyone without proper context. I gave the phone back.

"Satisfied?" she asked.

"For now. But I'm still going in with both eyes open." I turned south onto Route 29, and the wind whipped around my face as I cruised at the posted forty-miles-per-hour and ate my breakfast.

"Where are we going?" Charlotte asked.

CHAPTER EIGHTEEN

WASHINGTON EXECUTIVE AIRPORT is a public use, single-runway airport half an hour south of D.C. When I turned in, a Challenger 650 was already waiting with its engines running and the airstairs down.

I turned into a parking space, exited the car, and grabbed my belongings. I went inside the airport office, handed them my keys and asked if they had a spare bag that a passenger may have left behind. They were happy to hand over a well-used but clean leather bag with two metal clasps. I thanked them and brought it back to Charlotte, and she used it to quickly bag up all her belongings. She shut the trunk when she was done. "What about the rental car?" she asked.

"Someone will come pick it up. Let's go." I led the way across the runway and up the stairs. The pilot greeted us and waited until we were safely into the cabin before raising the stairs and returning to the cockpit.

Charlotte's eyes widened as she made her way farther in. It was a beautiful aircraft, with a wide cabin featuring dark polished wood set against the creamy beige of the leather seats. The spacious galley included an oven, microwave, sink, and a wardrobe for personal items. Executive seats featured 180°-swivel and reclining. Forward and aft bulkhead TVs offered access to every channel under the sun. The aircraft could easily fit ten passengers and since it was just the two of us, it felt all the roomier.

Charlotte set her bag down and turned to me with a twinkle in her eye. "You said you worked for *Homeland*? Any openings?"

I smiled. "This isn't my standard means of travel. I had to fly coach on the way up here." The truth was, the FID was funded by auditing wasteful projects throughout a dozen other agencies. Literally billions of dollars were misallocated or misused and budgets were shrunk elsewhere to give us the resources we needed without adding an additional burden to the taxpayer.

"Coach? Well, poor you." She took a seat and ran her fingertips across the supple leather. "Fancy."

"The bar is behind you if you want a drink. Help yourself."

I took a seat across from her and laid my chair back. The wheels were hardly off the ground when I closed my eyes and sleep took me with ease.

* * *

IT WAS JUST PRIOR to 1:00 PM when we touched down in Miami. A taxi was waiting for us and took Charlotte and me to the public parking garage where we loaded into my truck and set off for North Miami Beach.

The GRM offices were in a new two-story glass building that ran over fifty yards down the edge of Maule Lake. You could still see the lines in the grass from where the sod had been laid only weeks before, and the inside smelled like new construction: sheetrock, fresh paint, and lumber.

An enormous chandelier hung from a beam at the roof and down into the lobby's atrium. A wide, open staircase led to the second floor. Whatever GRM did, they were clearly experiencing success.

I approached the receptionist's desk. The young lady was talking with someone through a Bluetooth earpiece and she smiled at me as she raised a finger for me to wait. I grabbed a glossy brochure on the counter and flipped through it as I waited. It seemed that GRM catered to organizations with plump research budgets.

"Thank you for waiting," the receptionist said. "How may I help you?"

I set the brochure back down. "I'm Ryan Savage. Charlotte McCleary and I are here to see Mr. Tissot."

"I'll let him know you're here," she smiled. "Can I get you something to drink while you wait?"

"We're fine, thank you." I informed her of our names and she said that Jacques would be with us shortly.

We heard the click of shoes across the wood floor, and a man appeared from an adjacent hallway and started to make his way across the atrium. It was one of the men I had seen on the rooftop speaking with McCleary—the one I had pegged as French or Italian. He was dressed as well as he had been the night of the party, tailored suit, silk tie, and a matching pocket square. His black hair had a wet look, hung loosely over his ears and stopped before it reached his shoulders. His sharp nose seemed too long for his face and his eyes were a deep green. He smiled as he approached, "Hello, I am Jacques Tissot." He extended his hand to me, and then to Charlotte. "Thank you for coming," he said. "How was your flight?"

"Fine," I said.

He reached out and lightly touched Charlotte's arm. "I'm very sorry about your father, Charlotte. It's a terrible thing."

"Yes," she said, "Thank you. It is."

"Well, please, follow me. I am sure you have many questions, and I am eager to share with you what we found."

Charlotte stepped in beside me as he led us up the stairs.

"How long ago did you move into this building?" I asked.

"Just four months ago. We were at a smaller location up in Fort Lauderdale for many years, but last year we landed a long term contract with one of the largest hospital networks in the southwest and had enough capital to expand."

"What exactly does GRM do?" Charlotte asked.

We turned into a second-story conference room that overlooked the lake. A couple of kayakers were paddling over the water and beyond them, a small boy was sitting on a dock with a line in the water. His legs were dangling back-and-forth as he waited patiently for a bite.

Tissot extended a hand toward a couple of high-backed conference room chairs at the end of a long table. "Please, have a seat." He selected a chair opposite for himself.

"When a research lab," he began, "is tied to a large university for funding, or one specific government agency, then politics and differing agendas can often get in the way of innovation. GRM has privatized research, which allows our scientists the freedom to pursue research that might be considered unfundable by a risk-averse research council. Our clients are as wide-ranging as the United Nations and large foundations looking for flexible and efficient means to improve the soil conditions in third-world countries or the effectiveness of vaccines for ailments that affect those same regions—things like malaria, HIV, and respiratory diseases."

"How did my father come across GRM?" Charlotte asked.

"To be quite honest, I do not know. We do have a small department that caters to the general public. It typically caters to lawyers whose cases are in need of independent testing or verification."

Tissot was interrupted by another man entering the room. I recognized him at once as the other man on the rooftop, the one who had worn a frumpy suit and unkempt hair. Now he wore khaki pants and a polo shirt beneath a white lab coat. A file folder was tucked beneath his arm. His hair still looked as though he had burned his combs.

"Ryan and Charlotte," Tissot said, "let me introduce you to Dr. Edward Nance."

I stood, reached across the table, and shook his hand. Charlotte did as well, and we took our seats again. Dr. Nance looked a mixture of excitement and concern. He smiled quickly at us and murmured a hello before grabbing a remote from the table and pointing it at a TV mounted on the wall at the end of the table. We swiveled in our chairs to get a better view.

"Dr. Nance is one of our leading researchers," Tissot offered as the TV came on. "He has degrees from Johns Hopkins and MIT. Initially, I had put one of our junior researchers on analyzing the data that was on your father's laptop. But once we began to understand what we were looking at, I moved the project over to Dr. Nance."

"So what did you find?" Charlotte asked.

"Okay," Nance began. "So I received the laptop late yesterday morning, and it took me several hours to work through the science inherent in the data." Nance shook his head as though he were dumbfounded. "What Mr. McCleary had on there is utterly striking." Nance pressed a button on the remote and a mathematical formula appeared. The bottom part of it was circled. I never had been much of a math guy so it was all Greek to me. He switched to another image: the title page for a research paper. The next slide was a second formula that seemed to be setting forth proofs for whatever science was being laid out. Nance set the remote down and turned to us. "I don't expect you to understand all that," he said, "but I wanted to show it to you because it's absolutely incredible. What we have here is the ability to manipulate the amygdala—that's the part of the brain that processes your emotions—while controlling serotonin levels and providing a cognitive uplift. At least, in theory."

Tissot smiled at his eager scientist. "What Dr. Nance is trying to say is that this could rid humans of depression while at the same time greatly enhancing our mental functions. Each area of our brain is always functioning, but only at about fifteen percent of its capacity. This formula, should it prove itself, could allow us to double our cognitive processing while keeping our emotions from interfering."

"Of course," Nance said, "there would have to be years of tests and trials, but the foundation is there. This... this is huge. It could have literally thousands of applications from how effective we are on a daily basis, to the way we respond to trauma and the lingering effects of depression."

A middle-aged lady in a business suit rapped lightly on the door and poked her head in. "I'm sorry to interrupt," she said, looking at Tissot, "but you have an urgent phone call." Tissot stood up and excused himself, promising to return promptly.

I looked to Dr. Nance. "Are there names of any scientists associated with this data?"

The question sent a frustrated look into his face. "No. And that's the strange thing. I don't know if Mr. McCleary had an early edition of the research, but there are no names on any of this. Just the research itself."

Charlotte leaned forward in her chair. "Did my father tell you how he came across this? How it ended up on his laptop to begin with?"

"No," Nance replied. "He simply asked us to take it and provide him with our unbiased opinion of the data. Unfortunately, we don't know who this research belongs to."

I was pretty sure I knew. Douglas Peterson had told me that a Dr. Parker had taken his research findings from his time at DARPA over to MercoKline.

"If all this is what I think it is, then whoever controls this formula within the marketplace would be sitting on a gold mine of boundless proportions. It may," he said, now looking at Charlotte, "serve to explain your father's death. Maybe someone is trying to get it back after finding out he had all this."

Tissot reappeared and stepped into the conference room looking pensive. He returned to his previous chair and shook his head. He was lost in thought.

"Something wrong?" I asked.

"I… just received a very strange phone call. The caller indicated that they were with Pursuant Services and asked if we were finished with Mr. McCleary's computer."

I looked to Charlotte for an answer. "No," she said sternly, "that can't be right. My dad's partner at Pursuant is in Asia right now—Travis Barlow. He's finishing up a case he's been working with NCIS. Travis certainly wouldn't have called you without talking to me about it first. Did the caller give you a name?"

"No, he didn't. I asked for one, but he hung up."

Charlotte pinched at the bridge of her nose and closed her eyes for a moment. "I can't believe this," she said. "How is it that we know so little and someone else keeps staying one step ahead?"

"They're one step behind on this one," I said. "Can GRM turn the computer over to Charlotte?"

"Yes," Nance replied. "We can. I'll meet you downstairs with it. I'll need to go down the hall and get it from the lab. Miss Charlotte, I'll need to see your ID before I release it to you."

We all stood up and made our leave from the conference room. Dr. Nance disappeared around a corner, and Charlotte and I followed Tissot back down the steps to the front lobby. I turned to face him. "It might be wise for you to hire some expert security until I can figure out what's going on. Like I told you on the phone earlier today, Charlotte was almost killed last night because someone is trying to keep the information on that computer off the streets."

"A good idea, Mr. Savage. Thank you."

Dr. Nance reappeared with a MacBook in his hands. Charlotte presented her ID, and he handed it over. We thanked both men and returned to my truck. As we pulled out and started the drive south I continued searching for a tail. That call back at GRM asking for the laptop did nothing but keep me on high alert.

I was certain that the formula Dr. Nance had just revealed to us had originated from Dr. Parker's research. And I was certain that Douglas Peterson was killed last night to cover up details surrounding it. But I still didn't understand why someone would go through all this trouble to cover up a patent that Parker had chosen to take to a private company. He had clearly broken some big rules by not keeping his research within DARPA's walls, but that was nothing that a well-paid team of the right lawyers couldn't make go away.

There were still plenty of missing pieces and I was beginning to run out of patience.

I merged onto the Ronald Reagan Turnpike and headed south. Charlotte sat in the passenger seat staring out the window. "Do you have anyone you can go stay with until I figure this out?" I asked her.

"I have a cousin out in Phoenix. I don't think anyone would look for me there. But honestly, I don't want to be that far away from the investigation. I'd rather hang around here until we figure out what's going on."

"I can get my boss to book you a hotel in Miami, under an alternate name. Or you can come back with me to Key Largo. I have a friend I'm sure you could stay with. I would offer for you to stay at my place, but if the wrong person picks up on the fact that I'm working this case, I don't want you getting caught in the crossfire again."

"I don't know that I'm ready to spend a night alone yet—not after last night. I wouldn't mind staying with a friend of yours."

"I'll get you connected," I said. "We'll be at my office in about two hours. After that, it's beer-thirty."

CHAPTER NINETEEN

THE CHAIN CAUGHT, and I waited for the steel gate to slide away before driving into my office's parking lot. I parked, grabbed William McCleary's computer, and stepped out of the truck. "I'll be back as soon as I can," I told Charlotte. "There's a seawall over there if you want to stretch your legs and take in the view."

"Thanks, I might do that." I stepped back to shut the door. "Ryan?"

"Yeah?"

"Thank you for everything you've done. Everything you are doing. It means a lot."

"I'll be back soon." I shut the door and went inside, making my way down the first-floor hallway toward the evidence locker. I stopped when I saw a sliver of light coming from beneath Spam's door. I rapped on it and opened it. Spam was the FID's IT expert. He was a whiz when it came to computers, the internet, or hacking into programs or servers. His desk was facing the door. Several empty cans of Diet Coke were strewn across it, and a congested band of wires and cords ran down to the floor and over to a bank of servers and routers and other gadgets that were completely foreign to me. A poster of Luke Skywalker standing face-to-face with Darth Vader hung—a little lopsided—on the wall behind him.

He looked up from one of five computer screens and brushed back a lock of red hair that had fallen over his eyes. "Ryan! What are you doing down here on a Sunday? Shouldn't you be on a boat with a line in the water?"

"I was going to ask you the same thing. Shouldn't you be at home playing Zelda, or Call of Duty or something?"

"Yes," he said. "I totally should be. But my boss up at headquarters sent me a program he needs encrypted by tomorrow."

I held up the laptop. "Can you take a look at this for me? I need you to scour this computer and segment all the information on it. Emails, notes, documents, and the like." I handed it across his desk.

"A MacBook? Sure. Piece of cake. When do you need it by?"

"As soon as possible."

"I can have it done by tomorrow at the latest. If I have it finished today, I'll call you."

"Thank, Spam. I don't care what Brad says about you. You're a good man."

"Wait. What's Brad say about me?"

I grinned and stepped back toward the door. "Thanks again, Spam." I shut his door and took my exit of the building. Charlotte was sitting on the seawall, looking down at the water lapping just below her feet. I walked across the lush grass and came up beside her. "Hey," I said.

She sniffed and looked away.

"You okay?"

"I can't believe he's gone." A breeze tickled a few strands of hair off her shoulders and rustled the palm fronds above our heads.

I let out a long sigh. "Yeah," I sighed. "I can't either."

"Earlier, you said something about a beer?"

"Damn right I did." I held out my hand and helped her to her feet. "Let's go."

CHAPTER TWENTY

MY FEET CRUNCHED over the broken shells of The Reef's parking lot as I made my way to the door. Key Largo was a far cry from Miami, where the hum of traffic never stopped filtering through the air, functioning as an internal background noise. Out here, the silence was easy to recognize and appreciate. It wasn't unusual to take a morning jog into the state park to find yourself nearly convinced that you were the only person on the island. It wasn't a challenge to find a cove to run your boat into and hear nothing but the wind or a critter moving about in the mangroves. It was my kind of place. Everyone else could keep their big cities and skyscrapers and traffic. For me, *this* was home.

I opened the door for Charlotte and followed her in. The restaurant was unusually crowded for an early Sunday night. The bar was mostly empty and a couple dozen people were assembled on the back deck. The tables and chairs had been pulled back and everyone was standing along a line looking down near their feet.

Roscoe was behind the bar drying off clean glasses with a bar towel. "Ryan, there you are!"

"What's going over there?" I asked. "Someone pass out?"

His large chest shuddered as he chuckled. "No. It's the first annual, and possibly the last annual, Wayward Reef iguana race. Don Berry asked if they could use The Reef for some races. I said sure, but I'd better not come in tomorrow morning to have a lizard staring at me from some perch above the bar. Who's this pretty thing you have with you?"

"Roscoe, this is Charlotte. Charlotte, Roscoe."

He wiped his hands on the towel and came around to the front. He reached out and shook her hand. "A pleasure, young lady. How do you know this guy?"

She smiled half-heartedly. "It's kind of a long story."

"And I can see you would rather not talk about it. What kind of beer do you like?"

"Anything?" she replied.

"I have lots of anything. Give me a second and I'll get you something to wash your cares away." He returned to the bar and poured a couple of drinks from the tap, then set the glasses on the counter. "Here we go. Two Clamshell IPA's. Guaranteed to make you feel better by the time you reach the bottom."

I took them and handed one to Charlotte. "Thanks, Roscoe." A loud cheer erupted from the deck, followed by a riot of laughter and groans. We walked over just as everyone started to disperse. I saw Brad bend over and pick something up. When he turned around a green iguana was laying across his forearm. Brad saw me and came over, looking disheartened.

I nodded toward the reptile. "Since when do you own an iguana?"

"Since about three hours ago. I was coming back from Key West and Roscoe called to tell me to come by, that there were going to be some iguana races. So I stopped off at a pet store in Big Pine Key and got this loser. Apparently, there are such things as semi-professional iguanas who race for a living and have sponsorships. This guy just parked at the starting line like he expected me to hand-feed him." He looked to Charlotte and smiled like a used car salesman. "Hi, I'm Brad. Wanna buy an iguana? He's potty trained and his shots are all up to date."

Charlotte laughed. "No, thank you."

"Potty trained?" I said.

He glanced at me conspiratorially and shook his head. Roscoe came up behind Brad and clapped a meaty hand on his shoulder. "When I told you to come see the races, I didn't think you would actually enter a damn lizard."

"It sounded cool." Brad looked to the reptile on his arm. "But I didn't know you could buy a *dud*."

I excused myself when I saw Amy step out of the kitchen. I took her to the side and gave her the highlights of Charlotte's situation before asking if Charlotte could stay with her for a few nights or until we made some more progress on the case.

"Of course," she said. I brought her to Charlotte and performed the necessary introductions before leaving the two of them to talk. I returned to the bar and continued working on my drink. Brad followed me over and placed the reptile on the stool between us. It was a little strange trying to relax and enjoy my beer while being stared down by a creepy looking reptile.

"So," Brad said, "Kathleen called me and said she's putting me on this case with you because you're in dire need of more brainpower."

"I think she said she wanted to put another hurdle in front of me."

"Ryan, how is more smarts a hurdle? See? That's exactly what I mean."

"I'll get you up to speed on everything at the office tomorrow. Right now, I'm checked out."

The iguana's back legs suddenly slipped off the stool, and it dug its front nails into the stool's padding as it slowly lost the fight and moved toward the ground. "You going to help it out?" I asked.

Brad sighed and stared indifferently at it. "I guess."

CHAPTER TWENTY-ONE

I woke up to the familiarity of my own bed the next morning. After rolling out of bed and knocking out my typical regimen of push-ups and sit-ups, I made some coffee and went up to the upper deck of my houseboat, where I sat into a wooden Adirondack chair. A fiery orange sun was emerging from the Atlantic and a half dozen brown pelicans were diving on a school of baitfish not ten yards off my bow.

I had slept well last night with the confidence that Charlotte was safe for the time being. She and Amy had seemed to hit it off well last night. Amy was as skilled as anyone I knew at the helm of a boat, and she said she would take Charlotte out on the water today and try to keep her mind off the surrounding chaos. I was anxious to start connecting the dots, to understand who had sent those men after her and her father, and just what was going on with this research that Dr. Parker had produced.

Finishing my coffee, I went back down and took a shower before getting dressed and heading to the office. Brad's

Jeep Gladiator was already in the parking lot, but when I got upstairs, he was nowhere to be seen. I scooted my chair in, opened my laptop, and typed in my password. I reached down and opened my bottom desk drawer and flinched back when I saw a reptile staring back at me. From the back of the room, I could hear Brad enjoying a fit of laughter. I turned to see him and one of our lab techs doubled over.

"Hey," I said. "You know how you said this stupid thing is potty trained? Well, you have a mess to clean up in my drawer."

That dried his laughter up. He came over and looked in, swearing under his breath. "Bad Brad," he said.

"Wait a minute. You named your iguana after yourself?"

"No," he snapped. "That would be dumb. My grandfather's name was Brad. I named it after him."

I struggled to see the difference. "Can you get this cleaned up so we can get some actual work done?"

After locating a spray bottle and a roll of paper towels, it was another ten minutes before he was finished and the iguana was resting in a pet carrier on the side of his desk. The following half-hour was taken up with my recounting of the last two days, beginning with my meeting with Douglas Peterson and ending with my meeting at GRM with Jacques Tissot.

"Dude, I'm glad you're okay," Brad said. "And Charlotte. You still have no idea who's behind all this?"

"No. But there has to be a lot of money on the line. That, or someone is desperate to cover their tracks."

"So, what now?"

My desk phone rang and I snatched it up. "Hello?"

"Ryan, it's Spam. Are you at the office yet?"

"Spam, you just called my desk phone."

"Oh. Right. Come to my office. I've got everything you asked for. And then some."

I hung up. "Spam has something," I said. "I'm heading downstairs."

"I'll be right behind you. I need to do something real quick."

* * *

THE DOOR TO Spam's office was open, and I went right in. "Ryan," he said, "have a seat." The only chair I saw was sitting against the wall with a stack of paperwork on it. "Oh. Sorry." He started to get up.

"Don't worry about it. Keep your seat. What do you have for me?"

"Okay, well, I ran a program that did what you asked. I had it search all the information on your friend's laptop and then segment it according to topic and date accessed. Mostly it was emails, a few pictures, and the rest were documents. No videos and no hidden files."

Brad stepped in beside me and listened quietly.

Spam continued, "But Mr. McCleary had a file on someone else that, according to the system logs, he had spent a great deal of time looking at the two days leading up to his death. Those files are all about a Sergeant

Marcus Treadwell. Does that name mean anything to you?"

"No."

"He was in the Army for six years. Three of those as a Ranger and the last several months as a Delta operator. His file is basic enough, so I did some more digging through the Department of Defense's servers and discovered that Treadwell has another file that is classified top secret."

"Can you get into it?" I asked.

That got a dirty look from Spam. "Of course I can. But I'm not going to. You know what would happen to me if I got caught hacking into a DoD database and accessing a classified file?"

"They'd take away your access to Diet Coke?" Brad said.

"They would arrest me and throw me into a Supermax." Spam waved his hands. "No thanks." He turned back to a monitor and started typing. "So I did the next best thing and pulled what I could on Sergeant Treadwell's last couple of deployments. The first was when he was still a Ranger. He spent four months in Libya training locals there and maintaining peacekeeping efforts. His last deployment wasn't until eight months later, after he'd finished Delta training. He was in Afghanistan and it looks like he was sent out on a mission where two men in his troop didn't make it back. What's strange about this is that I can't see who was in his troop. His is the only name."

"Is he still with Delta?" I asked.

"No. No, see that's the thing. I don't know what happened on that mission, but Treadwell came back stateside right after and left the Army. Your friend, Mr. McCleary, had something on here that connected Treadwell with a company called MercoKline. Which I think is a major pharmaceutical company."

I felt the hair on the back of my neck stand up. "What was the designation on his discharge?"

"Let me see..." Spam fingers danced over his keyboard. "Honorable."

That didn't fit at all. It would have made sense if he had gotten badly wounded in combat; that would have qualified him to be medically discharged. It also would have made sense if he would have done something against the military code of conduct, something that would have slapped him with a dishonorable discharge. But for a new Delta operator to just be allowed to walk away? He would have owed the Army at least four more years after all that training.

"Where can we find Sergeant Treadwell?" Brad asked.

Spam leaned back in his chair and tossed his hands out. "I wondered the same thing. And the answer is, I don't know. He has no living relatives and five months ago he went dark. No job, no banking transactions, and no cell phone. He broke the rental contract on his house and fell off the face of the earth." Spam leaned back in, snatched a flash drive off his desk, and handed it to me. "Everything's on there. Including everything I could find on him. Maybe you can find a nugget in there that I missed."

"Thanks, Spam. This is really great," I said. "Do you have the computer?"

"Yes." He leaned down and grabbed it off the floor near his feet. "Here you go."

I thanked him again and Brad followed me down the hall, past the lab, and to the evidence room. I scanned my badge on the reader and went in, found an empty locker, and placed the computer inside. The electronic lock hummed as it moved into place and I entered a six-digit code on the keypad. No one would be able to access it without the code.

We left the secure room and started back down the hall. I punched the elevator's call button and stepped in when the doors opened. "What do you think all that means?" Brad asked. "You think that maybe whatever Dr. Parker came up with at DARPA ended up being administered to our guys in the field?"

"Yeah," I said. "I think that's a fair bet. Nothing else makes sense." I could think of no other reason why McCleary would have been looking into Marcus Treadwell. Something had happened in Afghanistan, and someone thought it best to keep it hidden away beneath a top-secret designation. We reached the stairwell and started up. "I think our next step is finding out where he disappeared to," I said.

We reached the second floor and had just stepped out when Kathleen appeared in her office doorway and motioned us over. We stepped inside and she told us to shut the door. We did as we were told and then watched Kathleen remove her glasses and rub at her eyes with the heels of her hands. She returned her glasses to her face and gave us a hardened smile. "I've got some news you're not going to like," she said. "So I'll just get right to it. My boss just called me from D.C. The Homeland's deputy director ordered him to have us stand down from the investigation.

He said it's being moved beneath the purview of another agency."

My fingers slowly curled into fists.

"How does anyone that high up even know we're on this case yet?" Brad said. "It's only been a couple of days."

"Probably because they had to clean up two different bodies and a car wreck for me last night," I said. "And Kathleen booked me a charter back to Miami."

"Oh."

"And because you're logging your case reports. Right, gentlemen?"

"Yes, ma'am," we lied in unison.

"So to clarify," I said, "you're saying we can't work this case anymore. I just walk away from what we clearly know is a conspiracy that someone is doing their damndest to cover up?"

"Officially, yes. That's exactly what I'm saying. You both are off the McCleary case. Don't work it in any way."

I'd worked with Kathleen for two years now and I knew that she would be just as angry as I was about a decision like that. No one likes a hot case to be ripped out of the hands of one of their investigators.

I also knew that the odds were that her boss, or even Homeland's deputy director, was in on the cover-up. He was simply another Washington bureaucrat who was getting political pressure from someone above him to turn the other way. He wouldn't be complicit, only negligent— failing to follow up and ensure that the case really did get picked up by another agency that was dedicated to seeing justice and truth prevail.

Officially… That's what Kathleen had said. I looked her square in the eye. My jaw was set hard, my tone angry and clipped. "But unofficially?"

"Unofficially, you sure as hell better wrap all this up and make some heads roll."

I relaxed a little in my chair.

"Kathleen?"

"Yes, Brad?"

"Since you're not married, would it be wrong for me to kiss you right now?"

"Yes. So don't try it." She was clearly keeping a smile under wraps.

"I think he's trying to tell you that we love you," I said.

"If either of you fails to tread lightly, if I get a call from my boss because he's heard rumors that you're still on this case, it's *your* heads that are going to roll. Don't make me look like a fool with this."

"We won't," I said. "That's a promise."

"Get out of here and get to work."

I knew we were going to have to watch every step we made from here on out. Even without the FID's support, I was as committed as ever to bringing an end to this chaos. My singular focus was unchanged: I needed to find Marcus Treadwell. And I needed to do it soon.

I had just returned to my desk when I heard Kathleen's angry voice ring out across the floor. "*Brad!*"

I paused and looked at him. "Tell me you didn't put that stupid iguana in our boss's desk."

He grinned nervously. "Maybe?"

I gathered up my laptop and headed back toward the elevator. "You're on your own there, brother."

CHAPTER TWENTY-TWO

U.S. ARMY MAJOR General Benjamin Sheldon listened half-heartedly as Rear Admiral Samuel Jensen continued to wax long about the merits of increasing the contingency operations budget. Sheldon looked around the conference table and was not surprised to see the room offering the Admiral only half its attention. Greta Sinclair was studying her fake, perfectly polished nails; Harry Custer was losing an obvious fight to keep his eyelids more than halfway open; even Colonel George Merryman was giving the table a long stare. These individuals were but a representative portion of all those in desperate need of stimulation, stuffed into the guts of the Pentagon, where windowless conference rooms were as common as classrooms in your average elementary school.

Sheldon stifled a yawn and checked his wristwatch. If the Admiral didn't put a lid on it within the next three minutes, then Sheldon was going to dismiss himself. Some forms of torture could not be endured. And soon enough, he wouldn't have to anymore. He had only seven months until he turned sixty-two, the mandatory retirement age for a two-star general. After that, the only meetings he would ever sit in on again would be those for the board of directors of a major corporation.

The meeting finally broke and after shaking a couple of hands, the general left the room. The heels of his black dress shoes echoed across the long corridor of the Pentagon's "E" ring. He turned into an open, outer office where his secretary was typing at her desk. She looked up over the rim of her glasses. "General."

"Lydia. I have a lunch meeting to get to. Colonel Wilson should be stopping by with my notes for the press briefing tomorrow. If I miss him, let him know that I'll follow up with him tomorrow."

"Certainly will." She returned to her typing.

General Sheldon went back down the corridor, took the elevator to the ground floor, and exited the world's largest office building through a side entrance where his Jaguar XJR575 was parked in a reserved space. The car was a charcoal gray, and its assertive styling perfectly matched his personality. The vehicle featured an imposing, upright front grille with mesh detail, full LED headlights, and eye-catching tail lights with a distinctive pinstripe.

Sheldon got in and set his foot on the brake pedal. He pressed the button to start the car and the 5.0-liter supercharged 575 horsepower V8 roared to life, echoing back the sense of power that he craved from life.

He backed out of the space, drove out past the security checkpoint, and finally merged onto Interstate 395, where he took it southwest into Alexandria. He was home in less than ten minutes, pulling into the stone-paved semicircle that sat proudly in front of his stately house.

The house was the one thing that he had gotten out of the divorce. It was the only thing he had really wanted; he let Margie have the condo in Honolulu and seventy percent of their sizable investment portfolio. The house was beautiful, and one that, after more than three decades of moving with the military, he finally considered to be home. It was built in the old Colonial-style: deep red brick, a pediment supported by two pilasters covering the porch, and double-hung windows accented with black shutters.

Margie had left him two years ago for a man ten years younger, only a few months after his Senate confirmation had placed another star on his shoulder, giving him his current position at the Pentagon. At the time, Margie's lover was running for Indiana senator. The chump had lost the race to the incumbent by more than a twenty percent margin. But Sheldon, he won out big. He didn't have to listen to his bitter hag of a wife peck his ear off anymore. The last two years had been the quietest of his life. He was a single man now, with retirement right around the corner and a deliciously ripe retirement plan on the horizon.

If his associates didn't screw it up.

A white Mercedes S-Class and a royal blue BMW 3 Series were already parked in the circle, and as Sheldon stepped out of his Jag and started walking toward the house, he noticed that the front door was open. He went up the steps and entered his foyer, then shut the door behind him. Low voices were coming from his office in the back of the house, and he made his way there.

Two men were in the study, both smiling as if Sheldon had just missed the end of a hearty joke. The first was a tall, well-built man with model good looks and the confidence to match. His hair was perfectly trimmed in the style of the day and he wore light gray trousers and a pink dress shirt with the top two buttons undone. John Brooks was forty-six years old and up until two years ago had been the general's brother-in-law. Even though Sheldon was nearly two decades Brooks's senior, the two men had always gotten along well, enjoying time together at the golf course or duck hunting in the Dakotas. When the divorce finalized, it did nothing to change their relationship. If anything, it served to strengthen it; Brooks was not a fan of his older sister either.

The second man was the youngest of the trio. Army Major Ted Dodson was, unlike the general, not in uniform. He wore blue shorts, a tropical shirt with a palm tree pattern, and tasseled loafers. His dark hair was cut short to military regulation and his eyes were set back deep beneath his brows. He sat on a leather couch with one leg crossed over the other. He had a drink in his hand.

Sheldon stepped across the rug and poured himself a scotch from the decanters sitting atop the sideboard.

Brooks was facing one of the well-stocked bookshelves built into the wall. His head was cocked to the side as he surveyed the titles. Sheldon had never been much of a reader. He had been in his early days, back when he thought they were helpful tools in a quest to rise in the military ranks. But by the time he had reached the rank of Lieutenant Colonel, he'd realized that a continual move upward rested solely on his political savvy. And he didn't need any books to hone that.

"I hope you don't mind, but I let myself in," Brooks said, still surveying the books. "Ted was already waiting outside."

Sheldon himself was a large man: wide shoulders, thick neck, and legs like tree trunks—a linebacker's body. He wasn't in the mood for banter and he didn't see how Brooks was in the mood to offer it. "I would like to know what's so funny," he said through gritted teeth. "If I knew you both had come for comedy hour, I would have rescheduled."

Brooks's lips drew a hard line. "Look, Ben, we—"

"No," Sheldon interrupted. "*You* look here. Both of you. This entire thing has gotten way out of hand. For nine months now everything has been fine. We cleaned up the whole Afghanistan mess and everything returned to business as usual. But now some guy at DARPA starts asking questions again and this entire thing starts to look like it's about to detonate in our faces." He extended his glass and shook it at Brooks. "You said you were going to fix this. And what do I get wind of? I hear that your man executes the rat in a public park. *A public park* for crying out loud!" Sheldon's face was taking on more red by the second. "And then he not only ends up dead in the offices of the very man he killed the night before, but his associate is shot up in a car chase. I could have picked one of a dozen former ex-special forces soldiers, each with a broken moral compass, to get this job done. But you said you had a guy you trusted. And look where we are now." Sheldon threw back the rest of his drink and started to pour another. "I've made sure that the team from Homeland was taken off the investigation. For now, we're in the clear. But if there are any more screw-ups...let me just tell you right now that I'm just about to run dry of political favors."

"Ben," Brooks said, "I know it looks bad. And you're right. My guys screwed it up. I don't know how someone started to work the angles so fast."

"Well, I do," Sheldon growled. "The someone is a Ryan Savage, an agent with Homeland. He was friends with that investigator. What was his—"

"McCleary," Major Dodson offered.

"Yes. McCleary," Sheldon said. "Savage doesn't think McCleary's death was an accident."

"How could he think that?" Brooks asked. "My guy inside the Miami PD said that the detective is going to rule it an accident."

"That doesn't matter," Sheldon said. "The reality is, if we don't keep a low profile we're going to lose everything we've worked toward these last two years and we're all going to end up in prison. Now, I don't know about you, but I didn't get into all of this to go to prison. Did we get McCleary's computer?"

"No," Dodson said. "It's at a firm in North Miami called GRM. We're trying to find a way in without raising any more suspicion. It's a high-tech research lab and security is pretty tight."

"Just leave it," Sheldon said. "Even if they find Dr. Parker's work they can't tie it back to us." He looked to Brooks. "Can they?"

"No. Absolutely not." Brooks said. "Besides, what they have is the previous version of the research. The one that went...wrong. Since you have the effects of that experiment buttoned up, we're in the clear."

"Okay." Sheldon took another long sip of his drink and seemed to cool. "What about the new formula?" Sheldon asked. "Where are we with that?"

"Good," Dodson said. "Parker said he's gotten all the kinks worked out and is ready to test it again. I'll fly out to Iraq next week and plan on administering it to a team of Green Berets."

Brooks was watching Sheldon's facial reaction. "It's fine, Ben. This time, he's got it. I've seen the lab tests myself. He knows where the science was wrong last time and has addressed the issues."

"If this fails," Sheldon said, "I can't cover up another body count like that. I don't care what Dodson's medical reports say."

Brooks smiled easily, the result of the bourbon settling into him and the bravado that came with being the senior vice president of MercoKline. "It's going to work, Ben. And when it does, we're all going to be extremely wealthy."

"And just so we're clear," Sheldon said, looking over at Dodson. "We're only testing it on three soldiers this time. Not *six*."

"Right. Also, I'm on leave all this week. I need to know if we're still on for our fishing trip, or if I need to reschedule."

"For now, yes, we're still on," Sheldon said. "But if I catch wind that someone is snooping around again, I'm not going fishing while the house burns down around us." He looked to Brooks. "I want to meet personally with Dr. Parker on my way to the Keys. I want him to look me in the eye and promise me that this time, there will be no mistakes."

"I'll set it up."

CHAPTER TWENTY-THREE

IT WAS JUST after eleven in the morning by the time I crossed the line into Orange County. I drove for another half hour before merging onto State Road 15 and taking it into Conway, a community southwest of Orlando. A sign up ahead read "Rosie's Diner" and I nudged the brakes and turned into their parking lot. I'd spent nearly five hours on the road and was hungry, tired, and ready to stretch my legs.

I got out and was quickly embraced by a hot blanket of humidity until walking into the diner where the heat was easily done away with by an overactive air conditioner. I waited at the front for someone to seat me. An older lady with a hard, weathered face finished taking a table's order and returned to the front.

"How many?"

"Just me," I said.

A stack of menus sat on top of a glass display that presented slices of fresh cherry pie, blueberry cobbler,

German chocolate cakes, and a pan of banana pudding topped with vanilla wafers. The waitress grabbed a menu. "Come on then."

She led me to a booth that looked out onto the parking lot. She set the menu down and slid it in front of me. "Breakfast is on the left; lunch is on the right. Today's lunch special is country fried steak. It comes with your choice of three sides and a roll or cornbread. You want something to drink?"

"Coffee would be great. And a glass of ice water."

"Lana will be over in a minute to take your order."

I opened the menu and looked it over. Rosie's offered the typical diner fare: breakfast with every possible way to combine eggs, bacon, sausage, ham, and pancakes. There were hash browns and biscuits and gravy as well. The lunch options included chicken fried steak, baked chicken, sliced roast beef, and a dozen different sandwiches and burgers. I decided I was in the mood for breakfast and, after settling a mental debate over an omelet or scrambled eggs, I chose the combination platter. I shut the menu just as a lady approached the table with my coffee and my water. She set them down and tugged out a straw from her apron, set it on the table.

"Hi," she said. "I'm Lana. I'll be your server today. What can I get you to eat?"

After I recited my order, she indicated to the end of the table. "Cream and sugar are over there. You want ketchup?"

"No, thank you."

"All right then. I'll be back."

She headed back to the front, and I responded to some emails and texts while I waited. When the food arrived, I took my time eating. Fifteen minutes later, the plate was clean and I was full. Lana returned to take my plate away, replacing it with a receipt that had a smiley face drawn on it. "I can take it at the register when you're ready. Is there anything else I can do for you?"

"Yes. To be honest, I came here to see you, Lana."

Her eyes narrowed. "Do I know you?"

"No. We've never met. I'm an investigator with the Federal Investigative Directorate, a division of Homeland Security."

"Am I in some sort of trouble?"

"No, not at all." I put on a disarming smile. "I wanted to know if I could ask you a few questions about your former fiancé, Marcus Treadwell."

She took a short, tentative step back. "Marcus? Why? What's he done?"

"Nothing," I said quickly. "He hasn't done anything. I'm trying to find out what really happened during his last deployment. I thought you might be able to help with that."

"If you came over here for answers, then you came to the wrong person. Marcus, he didn't tell me anything. I can send you away with plenty of cherry pie, but answers I don't have."

"I know you're in the middle of your shift. Do you think we could talk outside when you take your break? I just need a couple minutes. That's all."

Her jaw tightened and she looked away, shaking her head like she was mad at the world. "Hold on a minute." She left and disappeared into the kitchen. I was starting to think she had abandoned me when she reappeared and came back to the table. "I went ahead and took my break early. It's slow enough around here right now. Can I sit?"

I extended my hand across the table. "Please."

She slid in. She still looked angry. "Why do they have you out here asking me about Marcus?"

"We know that something happened while he was in Afghanistan. But the details of what exactly still aren't clear."

"All that happened almost a year ago now. Why are you just now coming around asking questions? It's a little late, don't you think?"

"It seems like the events of that night were buried. I'm trying to dig them up."

She huffed and looked away. "That's just like the government to miss something so glaringly obvious."

"Lana, I didn't mean that the events of that night were mishandled and forgotten. I mean that I think it was covered up."

She turned back to me and blinked. "What?"

"I'm completely in the dark here. That's why I need to know anything you think could help me get to the bottom of this."

She held up her left hand and pointed to it with her right. "We were engaged. When he called and said they were sending him home early, I was thrilled—we were getting married when he got back home from his last deployment. But as soon as I saw him walk back through my door, I knew he wasn't right. I tried for almost four months to get something out of him. Finally, he broke enough to tell me that two of their men had died and three were no longer fit for service. But he never told me why. He never told me *anything*. He just stopped talking and totally shut down." She looked out the window. Tears had started to rim her eyes. "I had to call off the engagement. I could have put up with just about anything. But him not talking, growing sullen and angrier every day, punching holes in the walls." She shook her head. "I couldn't do that. I couldn't help him if he wasn't going to open up."

"I'm sorry, Lana."

"You've got nothing to be sorry for."

"Did the Army give a reason why they discharged him?"

"They diagnosed him with acute PTSD, but for whatever reason, they didn't classify his situation as a medically related discharge."

"And you don't agree with that diagnosis."

"No—I mean, I don't know. Look, I'm a waitress for crying out loud. What do I know about how war can mess with your mind? I don't know what happened over there. Could it have given him PTSD? I'm sure of it. Happens to a lot of good men and women. But what I'm also sure of is that he was holding onto a secret that was eating him alive."

"Whatever happened in Afghanistan," I said, "I think he was under orders not to disclose it. Did you know the events of his last deployment are classified?"

"No. They are?"

"I want to help, but I can't do that unless I talk with Marcus and he tells me the truth. The problem is, I don't know where he is. I called his mother up in Charlotte but she swore she doesn't know."

"He didn't tell me where he was going."

I studied her for a moment. The flick of the eyes, the downward glance, the index finger picking at the thumb. "He didn't tell you," I said, "but you know where he is."

"He doesn't want anyone to know. If he did, he would have told someone. Marcus loved the military. All he ever dreamed of and all he ever wanted was to be a Delta operator. And he did it. He did what most men never could, and became the best of the best." Her face fell. "And then that was all taken away from him. And no one in the military or in D.C. had the balls to spend more than five minutes asking why two of our men were dead and three were in such bad shape they had to be medically unfit for service. And now you're here telling me it's a cover-up?"

"And if people like me keep hitting dead ends, then the truth will stay buried forever and Marcus will never get the healing he needs. Is that what you want for him?"

"No," she said. "Here, let me have your phone."

CHAPTER TWENTY-FOUR

THE FLORIDA EVERGLADES is the largest remaining subtropical wilderness in the United States, nearly two million acres of wetlands dominated by mangrove forests, sawgrass marshes, and wet prairies. I kept my hand on the tiller as I worked my way up a narrow inlet and deeper into the bowels of the untamed swamp. I had borrowed Roscoe's skiff for the trip. The fifteen-foot aluminum boat had a flat-bottom hull and a 75 horsepower outboard motor with a tiller arm control, perfect for navigating tree-choked swamps.

The sun was already low on the western horizon and the sky around me had started to dim substantially from the clear daylight it had been when I had entered the swamp a half hour ago. I continued inward, navigating the tangled web of waterways, all the while feeling increasingly isolated from the world. I passed a great egret wading through the dark water. It twisted its spindly neck and raised its head, looking at me in the same way I might look at Bigfoot.

There was a fair chance the bird had never seen a human before.

I swung the tiller to the right and the boat's bow curved left around a stand of cypress. The waterway straightened and I twisted the tiller and accelerated faster until I saw a hardwood hammock up ahead and made for it. The dry patch of land stood half a foot higher than the water and was choked with gumbo limbo and mahogany. I came in on idle and tied off on a thick tree root before cutting the engine and tossing my gear onto the dirt. I stepped out of the boat and navigated around a thick blanket of fern until I found a patch of dry leaves where I could drop my gear. The light was fading fast, so I got to work bringing out my camping hammock and fastened each end to the outstretched arm of a gumbo limbo tree. I suspended six feet off the ground; it would dip lower once I got into it and I didn't like the idea of only being a couple of feet off the ground. I ate some deer jerky, an apple, and downed some water for my dinner, then plucked out a lantern from my pack. I held down a button on the side, and when I released it five seconds later, the LED light started to flash in a rhythmic pattern. I hung it over a broken twig on the tree's trunk. That finished, I hung up my pack, grabbed a fixed blade knife and my .45, and climbed up the tree and slipped into my hammock. I adjusted my sleeping pad below me and then zipped up for the night.

I was tired. The events of the last few days had been powered by adrenaline and little sleep. I closed my eyes and listened to the sounds of the swamp: the chirp of crickets, the rhythmic croak of frogs, and the occasional hard, guttural squawk of the mangrove cuckoo. The symphony lulled me to sleep within minutes.

* * *

I woke to the sun's rays piercing through the canopy of leaves and branches above me. Somewhere a few birds sang quietly, almost as if they were scared to give away their presence to some predator. My muscles ached from spending all night immobilized, but I felt rested and recharged. All I could think of for the present was unzipping my cocoon and getting my feet on the ground. I pinched at the zipper and slid it down toward my feet, then reached up to the branch above my head and pulled myself into a sitting position.

Below me, several feet from my tree, a man was sitting cross-legged on the soft ground. He wore tattered jeans and a dirty AC/DC T-shirt over a slender but muscular frame. His beard was thick and bushy and tendrils of scraggly brown hair reached nearly to his shoulders. His wrists sat on his knees, his hands drooping toward the ground, back straight, striking blue eyes staring at me like a hawk. A fixed-blade knife was stuck in the dirt in front of him.

The lantern was off the tree, sitting next to him, turned off. He plucked up the knife and waved it toward the lantern. "That was a cute little trick with the light. Was that your idea?"

"It was." Treadwell was a former Delta man, and I knew he would have been trained in morse code. Krugman, the FID's genius lab tech, had helped me program the lantern with a message blinking his name.

An untrusting smile broke over his face. "Well, here I am. I guess you're here to kill me." He said it matter-of-factly like he wasn't surprised or even the slightest bit bothered by it.

"No," I corrected. "I came out here to talk with you. That's all."

"You'll have to forgive my skepticism. Are you armed?"

"I have a tactical knife and my Glock up here."

"Why don't you toss them over here?"

I took hold of them and tossed them over. He gathered them and placed them behind him. "Come on down. I'm sure you're feeling a little stiff after a night in that thing."

I reached back up and lifted myself out of the hammock, then set the toe of my shoe against a lower branch and put my weight into it. I swung the rest of my body down and both feet landed simultaneously on the soft ground.

"Right there." Treadwell nodded to a thick limb that grew parallel to the ground. It was thicker than my torso. I took a seat. "How did you find me?" he asked.

"Lana."

His eyes narrowed. I couldn't tell if he was angry or surprised or both. "I guess that makes sense. She's about the only one who would know. What did you do to her?"

"I didn't do anything to her. She's working at the diner. I went up there yesterday and asked her if we could talk, just like I'm doing right now."

"I'm not sure how you think I can believe that."

"I've got a sat phone in my pack over there. You want to call her and check for yourself?"

I watched as he considered the offer, and he seemed to relax slightly, knowing that the option was available to him. "Maybe," he replied. "For now, what exactly are we here to discuss? I've stayed quiet, just like you guys asked." He tossed his hands out. "I'm here, in this glorious swamp. I don't know how much more quiet I could get."

"I'm not sure I know what you're talking about, Marcus."

He huffed indignantly. "Just who are you?"

"I'm an agent with Homeland. I'm looking into the events of your last deployment."

"Are you now? Since when is Uncle Sam interested in what happened over there? They were never interested before."

"There have been good people who have tried to sound an alarm. But to be honest, they keep dying. Someone is trying to cover all this up. I think you might be one of the only people with some answers. I need your help, Marcus."

"I can't help you," he said. "Whoever these people are, they're too powerful."

"So you're just going to live in the Glades for the rest of your life? What are you doing all the way back in here, anyway?"

"My dad used to take me camping out here when I was a kid. He made a sport out of catching snakes. Cottonmouth and rattlers mostly. It's one of the reasons I wanted to join Delta. I'm comfortable in nature. Except for the cold. I really hate being cold."

"So that's it? You're just going to eat gator meat for the rest of your life? Live off the grid and forget the world?"

"You think I like living out here?" he snapped. "I'm not a swamp rat. This place is the pits."

"Then let me help you. Help me understand what went down in Afghanistan." His shoulders slumped slightly, and he took a deep breath. He looked off into the distance and seemed to go somewhere I couldn't follow. "Marcus." He looked at me. "What really happened over there?"

CHAPTER TWENTY-FIVE

TREADWELL GRABBED UP HIS KNIFE, stood up, and walked to a bald cypress. He stuck the tip of his knife into the trunk and looked off toward the water. "My element was heading to a town to meet an informant who knew the whereabouts of a local insurgence leader. Our directive was to go in small, so we hoofed it over the mountain and came back down onto the desert floor. No helos, no Humvees. We hit our waypoint just after 2200 hours and I got in about five hours of shuteye before my Sergeant Major woke me so I could take my slot in the overwatch rotation."

Treadwell grew quiet for a couple of minutes. I watched his hands and his neck gradually tense as he thought back over the events that had changed his life forever. "I felt like someone had slipped me a few Benadryls," he continued. "I couldn't keep my eyes open at first. But I got up the hill and the cold air helped to keep me awake. Around 0500 I watched my commander, Major Archer, emerge from his sleeping bag and start to wander around like he was lost.

He looked like a drunk stumbling out of a bar. Then he threw up all over his boots and then clapped his hands over his ears, like this"—Treadwell imitated the action—"and started shaking his head like there was something inside it and he was trying to get it out. Then he started banging his head on this big rock. And he wouldn't stop. He just kept slamming his forehead into it like he was trying to crack *the rock*."

My stomach twisted as I continued to listen.

"Then Sergeant Major Carlson gets up and starts doing the exact same thing. He pukes, stumbles around, and starts hitting his head on a different rock. Then..." Treadwell drifted off. When he spoke again, his voice was thick, choked with grief and anger. "I watched my commander take out his sidearm and blow his own brains out. No hesitation at all, no second thoughts. He did it with the confident ease of someone shooting a target downrange. And then... then my Sergeant Major did it too. By the time Major Archer got out of his bag to the time they both were dead was no more than three minutes. Just like that, they were gone. I haven't seen worse things in a horror movie."

"I'm sorry, Marcus."

"Yeah... well. The rest of my element, they never stirred, never heard a thing. I called it in and when the birds came to get us, I had to help to carry them to the helos—all three of them. They didn't wake up until we got back to base."

"Lana said they were unfit for service after that?"

He nodded. "Coleman, Diaz, and Gaskin. Damn good men. They never were right after that night. When they woke up, they had the minds of an eight-year-old. Coleman's still in a psych ward in California. I was the only one who got off with no adverse effects. After the sleepiness wore off, I was fine."

"What was the formal diagnosis?"

"Acute PTSD," Treadwell said dryly. "That, and the after-effects of some bad booster shots we got before we deployed. The vaccines were routine, but they claimed something was defective in them. A 'bad batch' is what Major Dodson called them. And I never did get anything more than a rehashed version of those two explanations."

By the time Treadwell finished telling me the details of that abominable night, my blood was boiling. I looked down to see my hands curled into fists.

"So why did you leave the Army if you were all right?"

"I was scared. Something wasn't right. I started getting really angry, and that was affecting everything I did. Major Dodson recommended that I discharge. He said he was concerned that I might do something rash, something I'd regret. I didn't disagree with him, so I left. And they let me."

"So then why are you holed up here in the Everglades?" I asked.

"I started asking questions of my own, trying to figure out what really happened that night. But I kept hitting wall after wall. I even had my blood work taken by an independent doctor off-base. He couldn't find any traces of anything. It was after I went and visited Diaz at his place in Atlanta that I found an unaddressed note in my mailbox telling me to back off. But I was like 'screw that.' I wanted to know what they did to my troop. So I kept on—even went to the Delta commander and the J-SOC commanders with it. They heard me out, and I believe they meant well. They're good men. But all they could do was forward my concerns to people they trusted. Nothing ever came of it. Just the same explanations as before. One night I arrived back home from the bar to find a man sitting on my couch. He had a gun pointed loosely at me, like holding a firearm was the most natural thing to him. And he told me that if I didn't stop asking questions, or if I told anyone about the conversation we were having, then it would be all over."

"Why didn't you tell Lana any of this?"

"Because I didn't have any answers. It only would have scared her and she would have started asking questions and poking around too. I didn't want to do that to her." Treadwell tossed his hands out. "But our relationship ended up a casualty of it all anyway."

I asked Marcus to describe the man who came to his house.

"Average height. Black hair. He was clean-shaven. I'm pretty sure his eyes were blue, and he had a strong jawline. Why?"

"Because I killed him in D.C. two nights ago."

Treadwell slowly turned and looked at me. "What?"

"Whoever is running this show," I said, "he was their cleaner. He was the guy with the mop. Except he finally got sloppy. The night I killed him he murdered a man who worked in the Pentagon, and my former commander the night before that."

"Good lord."

"Marcus, I need a better way to reach you. I'm sure I'm going to have more questions for you as this investigation moves forward."

"I'll keep an eye on this tract of ground. If want to get in touch, come by at 3 PM. And come alone. You bring anyone else back with you, you'll never see me again." He left my weapons on the ground where he had laid them and disappeared into the brush.

I brought down my hammock and gathered my things. Five minutes later I was back in the skiff, navigating my way back to civilization, thinking through what I had just heard. They would have to kill me too, if they wanted the truth to stay covered up. Short of that, I wasn't going to stop until I had blown the doors off and exposed every person involved with this despicable crime.

My greatest obstacle was that I still didn't know who had used America's most elite soldiers as guinea pigs for their potential product.

But I knew just how to find out.

* * *

"THAT PISSES me off more than anything I think I've ever heard," Brad said. He was gripping his beer bottle so hard I thought it might burst. Brad and I were both former military, but he had spent years in MARSOC, and that gave him a true affinity for our special forces that even I couldn't possess. "And Sergeant Treadwell just went off the grid? He's living in the Everglades?"

"Yeah. He didn't want them coming after his ex-fiancée."

We were sharing my Boston Whaler's double-wide helm seat, bobbing in the water a mile off the coast. There were only a few stray wisps of clouds to the east; other than that the blue mantel of the sky was unbroken. I needed to clear my head and think, and there's no better way to do that than on the water with a cold drink in hand.

"What did you find on this Dr. Parker?" I asked.

"Wayne Parker," Brad said. "He works at MercoKline's lab, at their headquarters in Sarasota. From everything I can see he's a lead researcher in what they call their 'Special Project' division. Strangely enough, he's the only researcher in that department. I actually had to get Spam to help me with that bit of info."

"So I think we can conclude that whatever Parker concocted while he was at DARPA, he took it to MercoKline and they found some application for special forces soldiers. Only the test went wrong and they've been covering their tracks."

"Someone within MercoKline has to be connected to someone in the Armed Services," Brad said. "There's no other way to know the unit movements and deployments otherwise. And then there's the actual administering of the drug. Someone had to do that, which means they had to be close to the operators." He looked over at me. "What are you thinking?"

"I'm thinking that I need a place on the mainland that no one knows about. A secure place out in the woods. Know of anything?"

Brad smiled knowingly and bobbed his head. "As a matter of fact, I know just the place. Why… what do you have planned?"

CHAPTER TWENTY-SIX

HE TURNED the corner and saw the fire hydrant fifty yards down the sidewalk. He put on more speed until his forty-nine-year-old body was running at maximum speed. He turned the corner and stayed on the sidewalk as he reached the park on the far end of his neighborhood where intermittent streetlights punctuated the darkness. The muscles in his legs, already warm and loose from a lengthy run, were burning now, working as fast as they could go as he finished his route with his mind and body going all in.

As soon as he reached the fire hydrant he pulled up and transitioned into a fast walk: his cool-down period. After running three miles he always finished with a strong sprint. He could feel his heart thumping hard inside his chest and he blotted at the sweat on his forehead with the back of his wrist.

He had never been much of a runner, but the events of the last year had almost forced him to be. Over the past year, the stress had continued to mount, moving him closer and closer to the edge of a mental breakdown.

But he couldn't allow that to happen. He had to stay both physically and mentally strong; he couldn't afford to allow anything to blur the absolute clarity with which he had to greet each and every day.

Another runner was coming up on his left, and he moved to the right to give the other man a wide berth. They passed just beneath a street lamp and the runner smiled at him as he ran by, raising his hand in greeting. A second later he heard his name.

"Wayne Parker?"

He turned around. The runner had stopped and was looking at him expectantly.

"Dr. Wayne Parker?"

"Do I know you?"

The runner approached. "No, no you don't. But boy, do I know you." And before Parker could react, the man had snuck in behind him, grabbed a wrist, and leveraged his arm up. Parker's head went down as he bent at the waist. He gasped from the pain. "Please," he croaked. "What do you want?"

He heard the growl of an engine just before a truck suddenly whipped around the corner and squealed to a stop along the tapered curb. Parker's assailant opened the rear door and forced him into the back of the crew cab, barked at him to slide over, and then joined him inside the truck before shutting the door. The driver punched the accelerator, and the truck growled again as it jolted back into the road.

Parker grabbed at his aching arm. "Who—who are you?" he stammered. "What do you want?"

"I want you to take a nap. Are you tired?"

"What?"

His assailant brought up a large fist and sent it right into Parker's face. The doctor's head rocketed backward into the window glass and then rolled loosely on his shoulders before his chin came to rest on his chest.

* * *

BRAD GRIMACED as he shook his hand and rubbed at his knuckles. "Dude's got a bone structure made of granite," he grumbled. I watched in the rearview mirror as Brad grabbed a blue Walmart canvas bag and slid it over Parker's head.

"You're kidding me, right?"

"What?" he said. "It was all I could find. We work for Homeland. It's not like we kidnap people all the time and have a shelf full of black hoods in the weapons closet."

He had a point. "He can probably see through that," I said.

"He can't right now. He's sleeping."

CHAPTER TWENTY-SEVEN

I GRABBED another beer from the small refrigerator and returned to my seat at the circular pine table. Brad was sitting across from me examining his hand.

"You might want to hang up the badge and find a different line of work," I said. "If you can't even punch a guy's lights out without—"

"I'm fine. I just don't know why it hurts so bad. This is nuts."

Next to me, Wayne Parker stirred. He groaned beneath the canvas bag and his head listed to one side before his senses returned and he sat bolt upright. We had his hands tied behind his back. "Hello?" he called out weakly.

Brad looked at me. We were still wearing our ski masks, but I could see him grinning behind his.

"Hello?" Parker put a little more gusto into it this time. He struggled against his bonds for a while and then gave up.

"Hello!!"

Brad leaned in close to him. "Hiya."

Parker jerked in a fit of fright. "Who—who are you?"

Chuckling, I plucked the eco-friendly shopping bag off his head. The yellow lighting in the cabin wasn't bright, but he squinted nevertheless.

"Dr. Wayne Parker," I began. "You were out for a long time. I was starting to think that my associate here had hit you a little too hard."

He took in his surroundings. The small cabin was just two rooms—a bedroom with an adjoining bathroom, a living area with a kitchenette along another wall. No TV, not even a phone. It belonged to a Marine buddy that Brad had served with in the Corps. His old friend was still active duty, but he had inherited the place from his father and told Brad he was happy to let him use it whenever he wanted. Parker's eyes moved from the room, to me, and finally, to Brad, which is when his recognition flipped on. "You. You took me—"

"Yes. I took you," Brad replied. "Kidnapped you—call it what you will. But that's behind us now. We're here, and that's what matters."

"What do you want?"

"Thank you," I said. "I appreciate you asking. And since you asked, I will tell you." I took another swig of my beer and placed the bottle on the table. "I want to play a game. That's what I want. I say a name and you tell me what you know about that person. Fair enough?"

Parker didn't answer, only glared at me with nervous suspicion.

"Don't worry," Brad said, "this will all become very clear to you in just a second."

I looked at Parker and held his stare. "Douglas Peterson."

A brief look of panicked recognition passed into his face but faded as quickly as it came. He didn't answer.

"Douglas Peterson," I repeated.

"What does this have to do with me?" he blurted out.

I picked up my beer and held it up. "I've got all night. I've got a refrigerator full of these, a soft bed in the other room, and a cupboard full of canned tuna. Now, I'm not super partial to canned tuna, but I could manage."

"I think," Brad said, "that you should tell us what you know about Douglas Peterson. Because"—he jerked a thumb toward me—"he knows that you know him, and I know that you know him."

Parker finally broke beneath our expectant stares. "He was a colleague of mine when I worked at DARPA. You couldn't just send me an email and ask me that?"

"No," I said, "I couldn't. But let's continue. William McCleary."

He shook his head. "I've never heard of him."

"Charlotte McCleary."

"No."

"GRM Research."

"No—what is this?"

"Sergeant Marcus Treadwell."

Bingo. Parker's eyes flared momentarily, and the little color he had drained from his face. His eyes wouldn't meet ours and he stared at the tabletop.

"Sergeant Brice Coleman. Sergeant Reggie Diaz."

"Stop it."

"Sergeant Joseph Gaskin. Sergeant Major Hopper Carlson."

"*Stop it.*"

"Major Dennis Archer."

"*Stop! Stop it!*" Parker was trembling in his seat now. His eyes were a blaze of torment, and his chest was rising and falling as he struggled to catch his breath. It was a full two minutes before he calmed.

"You want to tell us what that was about?" Brad asked. I could hear the anger seated in his voice. "You want to tell us why hearing those names made you so upset?"

Parker swallowed hard. "Because... because... no, no I can't tell you."

"You can't tell us?" Brad let out an irritated chuckle. "You're a coward, you know that? And there's nothing more despicable on this planet than a coward."

"He's right," I said. "And we have a way of dealing with cowards." I stood up and walked to the other side of the room where a small duffle bag lay on the floor beside the wall. I brought out Brad's tactical knife. With a 7-inch steel blade and leather-wrapped handle, the KA-BAR had been used in every U.S. war since World War II. If you weren't the one holding it, it could easily be the most intimidating thing you ever encountered.

I unsheathed it and walked over to Parker. I set the tip of the blade against the top of his thigh. "Start talking."

He stared wide-eyed at the knife dimpling his skin. "I—I can't tell you."

"I'll do far worse to you than they will." I pressed down and the blade punctured his skin and entered his muscle. Parker screamed. I left the blade in place. It was in a centimeter, hardly enough to do major damage. "More?" I asked.

He shook his head.

"Then talk."

He shook his head again.

I pressed in on the knife and it slipped in further, severing the muscle and making its way toward the bone. Parker let out a blood-curdling scream. His face was bright red now and beads of sweat had popped up all along his forehead.

"Okay! Okay…."

I slipped the blade out and his body relaxed.

"You have five seconds to talk," I said. "Five...four...three...two—"

"I killed them!" Parker blurted out. "I killed them and I hurt them." His face pinched into a sob and his whole body shook as he began to cry. Brad and I watched him, disgusted but with far too many questions to just sit there and watch him wallow in self-pity.

"How?" I asked. "Were they your little petri dish, a few lab rats that you could test your science on?"

"Yes," he said quietly. "But it wasn't supposed to happen like that."

Now that Parker's voice was well-oiled, I set the knife on the table beside me and sat back down.

"Why don't you start at the beginning," Brad said. "And give us the full picture."

He swallowed and took in a deep breath. "At DARPA, I had been researching the effects of how certain amino acids bonded to a very specific protein, under certain conditions, and the effects of it on the cognitive center in the brain. What I was seeing was extraordinary and I started to understand just what I had discovered. It was groundbreaking. So instead of carrying on as usual, I started to alter my research logs so as not to leave a trail of my findings. And then I reached out to a drug company and pitched me coming to work for them and bringing my research with me."

"You got greedy," Brad said.

"Yes. John Brooks is the senior vice president at MercoK-line. I knew him from ten years ago when we both were on a softball league together. So I brought this to him directly. He offered me a great salary and a truckload of shares in the company, all with the condition that I keep my research quiet. Basically, I was working secretly for Brooks, trying to perfect the research and its practical uses."

"Let's dial in on that last part," I said. "Why test it on our soldiers? On our *best* soldiers?"

Parker's shoulders hung limply at his sides; his chin sagged toward his chest. He looked every part the defeated man. "That was Brooks's idea. He's a driven man—I guess that's how you get into the kind of position he has. All along I had envisioned a drug that might curb the way we experience depression, and even—forgive how this sounds—make us smarter. All my research showed that it could enhance our cognitive functions. But Brooks, as he studied my reports, saw something completely different. You see, depending on the way the drug is constructed, it can have certain negative effects. It's like this with any drug, of course. But what he saw buried in my research logs was a drug that could harm in subtle ways. He saw the market potential in *that*. MercoKline already makes billions off the treatment of PTSD. Where I saw a cure, Brooks saw a poison."

"Then all he had to do was provide the cure," I said.

"And MercoKline makes out in the market," Brad finished. A quick glance across the table and I saw that my best friend was smoldering. The Marine Raider was taking Parker's words extremely personal.

"Yes," Parker said. "It's basically a way to manufacture a synthetic version of PTSD—which is generally the result of not only experiencing terrible trauma but also the loss of a shared identity when you return home to those who weren't there and can't understand. We found a way to introduce this drug at the cognitive level, bypassing the endocrine system altogether. Brooks started with special forces soldiers because if they show signs of this new syndrome, this new synthetically induced PTSD, then no one is immune. From there he plans to take it to the everyday soldier."

"Unbelievable," I said. I wanted to haul off and knock that man's head clean off his shoulders with a single punch. I leaned in, getting my face closer to him, and lowered my voice into a snarl. "Did they bother to tell you what happened to those warriors whose names I listed off to you earlier?"

"Yes. They told me."

"And what did they tell you?"

"That a squad was on patrol in the desert and made camp for the night. That two of them never woke up and that three of them woke up with developmental issues. They said Treadwell was the only one who made it out without any negative long term effects."

"Two of them never woke up?" Brad muttered under his breath. "That's a big fat lie. Why don't I go ahead and share with you what really happened that night?"

Parker looked confused, as though it had never crossed his mind that he would have been lied to. "What do you mean?"

Brad proceeded to relay Treadwell's account of that night, how the two troop leaders had indeed woken up, how they had self-mutilated and then, finally, had taken their own lives. Brad told him about the other three warriors, how all three were suffering from various degrees of mental challenges to this day, and would most likely never recover.

"That's—that's not what they told me," Parker cried out.

"And yet, that's exactly what happened," I said. "Marcus Treadwell was scared out of his mind and left the only life he had ever wanted. And then, to top it off, his life was threatened in order to keep him quiet about any wrongdoing.

Parker was shaking his head now, a distant look on his face. His expression had turned into one of horror, and I could see true and honest guilt pouring out of him.

"So," I continued, "why don't you kindly share with us how in the hell you and Brooks got that drug into our boys to begin with?"

CHAPTER TWENTY-EIGHT

PARKER LOOKED LIKE AN ABUSED ANIMAL, utterly defeated and scared.

"I'm sorry," he finally said. "I'm so sorry."

"Save it," I said. "Everyone is sorry after they get caught. The way I see it, the way a jury is going to see it, you're just as complicit as everyone else."

"I swear, when I came to Brooks with the formula, I didn't know he would do something like that. I honestly thought we would be helping people with it. I just wanted to make sure that, since I was the one who discovered it, that I would profit from it. I didn't know he was going to flip the idea and go testing it on soldiers."

"And yet, when he proposed the idea, you went along with it. You didn't blow the whistle."

"No. I didn't." The admission came out in nearly a whisper.

"So I'll ask you again. Who got that drug into the men in that Delta element? Those soldiers aren't exactly accessible."

Parker didn't answer right away. It was like he was pondering that final step over the cliff. As if what he had said up to this point hadn't been enough to betray the cause. He closed his eyes. "There are others—two men, as far as I know—on the inside. Two Army officers. A Major General and a Major."

"*What?*"

"Yeah. I swear."

"No way," Brad snapped. "A two-star general isn't going to betray the service. Not like that."

"Maybe not your average two-star," Parker said. "But you do if your ex-brother-in-law is the senior vice president of MercoKline."

I stared at him. "You're kidding?"

"No. General Sheldon was married to Brooks's older sister for almost thirty years. They got divorced a couple years ago. Brooks brought his idea to Sheldon, and Sheldon found Major Dodson to administer it."

"Who does Dodson report to?" Brad asked.

"He's a doctor at JSOC."

My anger flared again. JSOC is the Joint Special Operations Command. It's headquartered at Fort Bragg and oversees all Special Missions Units, including DEVGRU—formally Seal Team 6—Delta, and the 75th Ranger Regimental.

"You want me to believe that a medical officer at JSOC administered what he knew to be a drug intended to harm our men?"

"How else would they have gotten it? Brooks offered him a lot of money, too."

"Hold on a minute," Brad said. "Let's say for a minute that you're telling the truth. And I'm not convinced that you are. But...if some Major did do that, then how did he get away with the chaos that resulted? There would have been an investigation."

"There was a preliminary investigation. Losing six guys like that hit JSOC hard. But the investigation came back inconclusive and the file was shut. Dodson leaked something about tainted vaccine boosters and that was that."

I crossed my arms over my chest. "They would have done autopsies. How did they not find anything in their systems?"

"Because the drug, it leaves no ash—no traces. Twelve hours after administering it, it looks like saline in your blood. And by then it's done all the damage."

"So that's it?" I said. "You all just shut up shop and tucked the project away until Douglas Peterson started asking questions again?"

Parker huffed and shook his head. "No. We didn't tuck the project away. We went back and reworked the science. We've got it this time. It's perfect and Dodson is taking this new batch to try on a few Green Berets after they ship out next week."

That last sentence sent a chill down my neck. "Again? You all are doing this again?" I didn't wait for an answer. I uncrossed my arms and sent my fist plowing into the side of Parker's face. His chair flew off to the side, toppling onto the hard pine floor where Parker landed with a grunt.

Brad and I left him where he was for five minutes, neither of us speaking, both of us wanting to tear the scientist limb from limb. It was Brad who finally picked him back up and set his chair aright.

I looked at Parker. His upper lip was caked with blood and his cheek was already swollen to the size of a softball. "I'm inclined to use that knife on you," I said. "Tell me what else I need to know."

Parker worked his jaw and grimaced. When he spoke again, his words had a lisp. "I've spent the last nine months reworking the initial formula. On the first try, I had failed to account for a genetic split from a synuclein variation—a protein in the brain. But the drug is perfect now. It will work the way Brooks wants it to. Also," Parker added, "I've got proof against Brooks about all this on email. I also have two short conversations on an audio file between me, Sheldon, and Dodson. It's on my laptop at home."

"So MercoKline has funded the research, but you and Brooks have kept it siloed from the other R&D departments?" Brad asked.

"Yes. I work alone in my own lab under his direct supervision."

"Where is the initial formula?" I asked. "Do you still have some?"

"Yes. It's at the lab. I've had to use it as a baseline for current research. It's in a secure refrigerator that can only be accessed by me or Brooks."

"When you go in to work," I said, "what does that process look like? How do you get into the lab?"

"What?"

"Did I stutter?"

"No. But why would you want to know that?"

"Because, Dr. Parker, you are going to help me break into MercoKline."

CHAPTER TWENTY-NINE

MERCOKLINE'S HEADQUARTERS was located in a seven-story building in the center of a sprawling fifty-acre campus. The building was brand new, with construction completed on it just last year. Each floor was offset from the one below it; it looked like two enormous staircases wrapped in glass. It was chic and modern, with an open atrium set between the two odd-looking towers. A forward-looking design that was everything you would expect from one of the largest companies in the United States.

I had spent the last twenty-four hours working on a plan to get me into the building without raising any suspicion. Kathleen's warning about keeping a low profile still rang in my ears. But my plan wasn't going to work unless I could get into that building.

I was driving north on Route 41 in a pearl white Cadillac CTS: Dr. Parker's car. I was alone. I had an earwig in, with Brad, Parker, and Spam on the other end; the former two at the cabin and Spam at his home office.

I had called Spam earlier in the day, updating him on the situation, that the FID was officially off the case, and could he help me off the record. He didn't hesitate to say yes and said he had everything he needed to assist me at home. Which was akin to saying that, since we couldn't use NASA to get to the moon, Spam had a command center, shuttle, and launch pad in his backyard. He had every gizmo and gadget you could imagine, an entire guest room stuffed with server racks and portable A/Cs to keep them cool. I had wondered more than once how he managed to pay for it all on a modest government salary. But I never bothered to ask him outright.

My earwig crackled and then his voice came through clearly. "Take your next left," he said. I could feel the tension building in my shoulders. This had to work. If it didn't, I ran the risk of showing our cards to the other side and not having a job when I returned to work. After reviewing the plans with Spam and meticulously planning the most achieved scenario, he said he put the odds of success somewhere in the low thirty percent range. I promptly told him that I wasn't interested in the odds. Brad just made it clear that he didn't want to go to jail.

"Your next turn," Spam said, "will put you and the car on their exterior cameras. Standby."

It was nearly midnight, when the building would be mostly deserted. Spam had spent the last several hours hacking into MercoKline's security cameras. He would be able to feed a loop into the system so that the security footage didn't show me coming or going from the build-ing. The catch was, he couldn't do it for more than eight minutes. Their system ran a check for such interferences on that interval. Spam, as good as he was, couldn't override it. I had eight minutes from the time he started the loop to drive onto the campus, get inside and through security, do what I needed, and then not only exit the building, but drive away so that the car was off their exterior camera facing the main street. I was driving Parker's car in the event that I couldn't get away from the building fast enough and the camera picked up the vehicle.

Thirty percent chance.

"Okay," he said. "Good luck, Tuna." I rolled my eyes at the name he'd given me for tonight's mission. "You'll take your next turn. Just before you come around the doctor's office on the corner, you'll be in view of their cameras. On my mark." I turned on my blinker and set my fingers on the edge of my watch. "Ready... M*ark*." I pressed the timer on my watch and started into the turn, accelerating down Merco Avenue, the main road that led up to the drug company's headquarters.

"Hold," Spam said, and then a few seconds later, "We're good. The feed's loop is in place. You have eight minutes. The security guard can see you on their monitors driving in, but it's not recording and it won't live on their servers."

I drove up to the massive building and navigated the Cadillac into a parking lot near the front. I turned the car off and got out, using a hurried stride to make my way across the sidewalk and to the front door. To blend right in, I was wearing dark slacks, a blue dress shirt, and a white lab coat.

I had spent some time with Parker, looking at floor plans of the building that Spam had provided. Parker walked me through each step of the entry process: where the security stations were, at what point to scan his badge, and exactly where I was going.

I entered at the front door and was immediately greeted by a security guard and a metal detector. Another guard was sitting behind a bank of monitors.

"Evening," he said.

"Good evening." I took out the contents of my pockets, in this case, the keys, a laminated badge with my photo on it, an aspirator, and my phone. I placed them in a plastic bowl and stepped through the metal detector with no problems. The guard set the bowl on the belt of an x-ray machine and pushed a button for it to start moving. The other guard watched a monitor as it passed through. Once it was on the other side, he gave me permission to retrieve my things.

The guard looked at my aspirator and shook his head. "I've got asthma something bad too. It got real bad there for a while where I thought I was going to have to quit my job here. But those little aspirators have saved my tail more than once."

"Me too," I said politely.

"You know, what's really bad is when I'm in a hurry. I can feel my chest start to wrap itself in its own grip. If I don't have my medicine, then I'm bound to go into one of those fits where I can't get a breath for a few minutes."

"Tuna," Spam said. "You don't have time to make new friends. Get moving."

"Tell me about it," I said and then started walking away. He looked like he was about to start saying something else but then didn't. "Have a good evening," I said over my shoulder.

"You've already burned ninety seconds," Spam said.

"I don't need a by-the-second countdown, Spam."

Brad's was the next voice I heard. "You have six minutes and twenty-two seconds."

I took a hallway to a set of double doors and scanned Parker's badge. I heard the latch click and pushed open the door, then took my next right. There was a heavy door at the end with a sign that warned of unauthorized access. I removed a piece of waxed paper the size of a credit card from the pocket of my lab coat. I worked my finger beneath a film of transparent plastic and peeled it off. I reached out to place it on the thumb scanner when I heard Parker's voice.

"Make sure you scan the badge before you try the scanner."

I pulled my hand back just as the plastic was sliding onto the scanner. My heart was beating a little faster now. I silently chastised myself for getting the order reversed. I lifted the badge and scanned it, then an orange diode on the thumb scanner turned on. I set Parker's thumb print on the glass and waited.

Nothing.

I shifted it around, careful not to smear the print.

Nothing.

"Spam?"

"Try flipping it over." He didn't sound very confident.

I did as he said and tried again. The diode moved from orange to green and gave two beeps. "Now," Parker said, "there's a keypad above the scanner. You'll need to enter my code. It's eight digits. You ready?" Neither he nor Brad could see me. Spam could, but Parker and Brad were only running audio out at the cabin.

Parker's guilt had seemed to steadily increase since our conversation last night. He kept saying he was sorry, that he should have done something. Finally, he offered to help by his own volition instead of us having to compel him by threat of further pain. I didn't really care that he wanted to help now. It was too late to make this right. Nine months too late.

"Ready," I said, and I punched in the code as he started to relay it to me.

"Zero-eight-two-two-seven-nine-zero-five."

The door latch gave and I pushed it open. I was in.

CHAPTER THIRTY

THE ROOM WAS MASSIVE.

The ceiling was over twenty feet high and all around me were stainless steel tables filled with beakers, microscopes, computers, centrifuges, and plenty of other equipment that was completely foreign to me. A massive irony was the American flag standing in a corner. It made my stomach curl.

The first thing I did was look around to make sure I was alone. Parker said that he was the only one who had access to this lab, but for obvious reasons he was pretty low on my trust meter. There were no cameras in this lab, and Spam would be blind to me while I was in here.

Seeing no one, I quickly located a box of latex gloves, snatched two, and slid them on. Then I made my way to a corner where a commercial, stainless steel refrigerator stood eight feet high. A keypad was on the front door, as well as another thumb scanner. "Okay," I said to Spam, "I'm at the refrigerator."

"Okay. I need the model number. Check the back."

Parker had informed us that, unlike with the lab itself, whenever this refrigerator was opened, Brooks received a private text message and email to notify him. Before I could open it, Spam had to jam the signal, but he couldn't do that without knowing the model number; the signal notification option was built into the fridge at the time of manufacturing.

I slid to the side and slipped my fingers into the half-inch space between the concrete wall and the back of the fridge. I pulled back. It didn't move. I braced myself and tried again, tugging back as hard as I could. Nothing. "Spam, I think it's bolted in. I can't get it to move."

"Okay. There might be one on the inside of the door." A brief silence as I rolled my eyes. "But I guess that doesn't help us much. Um...check the sides. Maybe nearer to the floor."

I got down on the floor and scanned the sides, looking for anything that might identify the model. Seeing nothing I moved around to the front and saw a thin, yellow strip of paper on the top edge of the air flow grate. "Got it."

"Go," Spam said.

I read it off to him and waited for an eternity. It didn't help that Brad thought the silence was a good time for another time check.

"Five minutes."

"Okay...you're good, Tuna. Go."

"Parker?" The scientist recited his code, which was different from the one used to access the lab. When I was finished punching it in, I scanned the thumb print and tugged on the door. It opened and bright LEDs illuminated the shelves within, which were filled with plastic cases and racks of tubes.

"Signal's jammed," Spam said. "Get your goodies and get out of there."

Peterson had told me to look for a red tube rack on the back of the second shelf. I slid a styrofoam box to the side and peered behind it.

"Parker, it's not here."

"What? Um...try the bottom shelf? It's a red one."

I squatted down and looked around a hard plastic case. A red vial rack was standing behind it. I slid it out and plucked out a vial, turned it on its side, and read off the label. "X8-Mamba-YST."

"That's it." Parker said. "That's the one. There should be nine of them."

There were nine of them, but I still couldn't help but be a little skeptical. "Parker, if you're lying to me—"

"I'm not. I swear."

"Where's the new batch?"

"On the inside door. In a small green case."

"Four minutes."

I located the green case and unlatched it, then removed a vial before returning the case to its place on the door. Next, I grabbed two vials of the first batch from the red tube rack and pushed it back.

I stepped back and shut the door.

"I've deactivated the entire signal," Spam said. "And reprogrammed the refrigerator's master chip. They won't be able to open it again." I heard a hint of satisfaction in his voice. "Not without me, anyway."

I located a small foam-molded hard case for the vials and put them in. I snapped the case shut and slid it into the pocket of my lab coat, peeled off the gloves, and did the same.

"Three minutes thirty," Brad said.

I moved to the main door and used the edge of the lab coat to open the door, then wiped the outside handle after I'd stepped back into the hall.

It was time to go.

I retraced the way I had come in, making my way down the hall and turning down another corridor. I nearly ran into a middle aged man in a security uniform.

"I'm sorry," I said and went to move around him.

He frowned at me and held up a hand. "Just a minute, please. It's a little late to be working in this wing, isn't it?"

"It is," I agreed. "I forgot something back at the lab and just came back to get it."

"Can I see your badge?"

"Of course." I handed it over and he rubbed his chin as he studied it. The nameplate on his chest read, "S. Myers."

"Doug Peterson?"

"Yes, sir. That's me."

"I don't remember approving you. Any new badges for access into R&D's A wing require approval from me."

I stared blankly at him. "I'm sorry. I'm not sure what you want me to say? I have a badge. I'm here on invitation from Dr. Parker."

"Wayne Parker?"

"That's the one." I smiled cordially. "Do you treat all of MercoKline's visiting scientists like they're here to steal company secrets?"

His face flushed red. "Don't act like it doesn't happen. Because it does. That's why I have a job. Now, come with me. I'm going to run you through the system myself. Where did you say you were visiting from?"

"I didn't."

"Okay, smartass. What organization do you represent?"

"Peterson Consultants. We're a private research company."

When I heard Spam's voice again, it was filled with urgency. "Ryan. You have under three minutes. You don't have time for this. You have to be out of that building and down the block in the next two minutes and fifty-three seconds." I could heat start to rise off my forehead. He was right. I didn't have time for this.

"Follow me," Myers said. He turned on his heels and started back down the hall. I fell in step and followed him down another hall before stopping and wheezing through my throat. My shoulders slumped, and Myers turned back to me.

I held up a finger and nodded in halting manner as I constricted my neck, making my face turn color. "As—asthma," I choked out. I wheezed in a short breath and made to steady myself.

Myers took a couple of steps toward me. He looked genuinely concerned. "Are you okay? Do you have an aspirator or anything?"

"Y—Yes." On cue, I reached into my right pocket and retrieved the inhaler. I set a palm on the wall and leaned over, still trying to suck in a breath.

Myers took another step and laid a hand on my back. "Doctor. Do you need me to get some help?"

I started breathing normally again. "No," I said. "But I appreciate your concern." I aimed the inhaler at his face and pressed down on the canister. I held my breath and stepped back as the tiny droplets plumed into his face and he sucked them in.

"What's going on?" he snapped. He started wiping at his face from where some of the spray had gotten him.

"You're going to sleep for a few minutes." The last word was hardly out of my mouth when his eyes shut and his chin started for his chest at the same time his knees buckled. I slid over to him and slowly laid him on the floor.

The inhaler had a sleeping agent in it. A proprietary concoction created by a very proud Krugman. I was told that its effects would last for up to fifteen minutes. The person would wake up and have no memory of the previous half hour before the sleeper was administered. So far, the sleeping part worked. Now I just hoped that the memory loss would too.

"Parker," I said, "I'm in a little bit of a hurry here. Where do I put Myers?"

"What did you do to him—ouch!"

I heard Brad mutter something to him.

"Okay," Parker said. "Where are you exactly?"

"I came out of the storage lab, turned left, and then took my second right. That's all I know."

"Okay, then you're not far from the A wing common room. This time of night there won't be anyone there. You can lay him on a couch."

"Tell me where to go." I checked both ends of the hall. No one was around, but that could change at any second. I really didn't want to have to use the spray again. One person waking up with a senior moment was one thing. But two people? That's when people started asking questions.

"At one end of the hall should be a dark gray door. See it?"

"I do."

"Head toward it. Before you reach it, on your right, you'll see a door marked, Kline Commons."

I stepped behind Myers, leaned down, and hooked my forearms behind his armpits. I heaved him up and the heels of his shoes squeaked along the floor as I walked backward down the hall. When I reached the door, I laid him back down and opened the door.

An open kitchenette lay at the far end, with a table and chairs sitting near a near-empty bookcase. There was a living room of sorts, with three brightly colored couches and a seventy or eighty inch TV mounted on the wall. It was on, tuned loudly to reruns of The Big Bang Theory.

There was no one there. I picked Myers up again and dragged him over to one of the couches where I laid him back down. I picked up his feet and set his legs out straight on the couch, then placed a decorative pillow under his head. For good measure I grabbed the TV remote off a side table and slipped it in between his fingers, then tucked his hand close to his side.

Satisfied, I checked the hall and, seeing it still empty, stepped out and pulled the door closed behind me. I turned left before reaching the lab and hadn't made it ten more paces before I heard a door open behind me and I heard someone call out.

"Ryan?"

I kept walking, not bothering to turn around.

Footfalls echoed across the walls as the individual behind me started coming faster. "Ryan!"

Who in the hell would know me here?

I whipped around and put on a false smile, prepared to reach for the inhaler again. I turned to face a middle-aged black man. He stopped when he saw me and his eyes narrowed. Then he smiled, as though embarrassed. I didn't recognize him. "I'm sorry," he said. "I thought you were someone else. Ryan in marketing. I was wondering what he was doing down here this time of night. Now I know. I'm sorry."

"No problem." I smiled politely and continued my course down the hall.

"Ryan," Spam said, "you have fifty-five seconds. I don't think you're going to make it."

I shouldered open the next door and turned right, moving from the linoleum to carpet. "Thanks, Spam. I don't need your commentary right now."

The hallway brought me back out to the lobby, and I moved quickly to the exit while trying not to attract attention from the security guard watching the monitors. A quick glance showed me that he was busy doing something on his phone. He never bothered to look up. I didn't see the guard who had spoken to me when I'd come in.

I stepped outside into the cool night air and started running once I got out of range of the glowing light at the front of the building.

"Fifteen seconds."

My keys were already in my hand and I unlocked the car as I reached it. I flung open the door, jumped inside, and had it started within a second. I backed up, threw the gear into drive, and shot out of the parking lot. I didn't bother with the stop sign at the main entrance and accelerated away from the building at sixty-miles-an-hour. I tapped the brakes at the next intersection and hung a quick right onto the main thoroughfare. The rear of the car fishtailed as I overturned and I righted it just as the medical center on the corner cut off my view.

"And...you're good," Spam said. "Exterior cameras are clear."

I looked over to the passenger seat where the satchel lay. As I slowed for a stop light, I reached into the lab coat and brought out the hard case. I flipped open the latch and looked in. The glass vials sparkled in the glow of the street lights. This was why William McCleary had been killed. This was why Douglas Peterson had been murdered as he walked beside me, why Charlotte had nearly been murdered that same night. It was how an entire Delta troop had been assaulted by two of their own officers.

The light switched to green, and I shut the case and placed it on the seat beside me.

I could feel my anger start to ebb.

Justice was now at my fingertips.

CHAPTER THIRTY-ONE

He loved Florida.

And in seven months he was going to move down here.

He wasn't exactly sure where yet. The Lower Keys, maybe. Perhaps Naples or even here, in Sarasota. Wherever he chose, he would be free to do as he pleased, with no timetables or calendars to consult. He might just throw his watch in the trash and go without. No more meetings, kissing the White House cabinet's ass, no overbearing wife —he would truly be a free man. And in a couple of years, when the company's stock soared through the roof, he would buy his very own island somewhere. Perhaps a multi-million dollar motoryacht like he was on right now.

General Benjamin Sheldon sat on the main deck of Brooks's yacht with a glass of scotch in hand. The water craft was moored in Sarasota Bay, giving Sheldon a clear view of Longboat Key in the distance. He took a sip of his drink just as Dodson appeared on deck, followed by the boat's owner.

"He hasn't shown yet?" Brooks asked.

"No," Sheldon replied. "Has anyone tried calling him again?"

"I did," Dodson said. "About five minutes ago. He's not answering."

The beautiful weather, the scotch, and the boat aside, Sheldon could feel himself start to get a little angry.

He and Dodson were on the threshold of a much-needed vacation. As planned, they had stopped by here to talk with Dr. Parker on their way down to Big Torch Key. He and Dodson had rented a two-room bungalow on a tiny island. For the next two days, they were going to fish, spend time with the right kind of ladies, and sleep in too late.

But Parker not showing was just a bad start to the fun.

Brooks, who was usually the most relaxed and level-headed person in the trio, seemed to be carrying around some anxiety of his own.

Dodson cleared his throat. "You don't think he would bail on us, do you?"

Brooks managed a crooked smile in response. "Not a chance. I've made it quite clear to him what would happen should he ever try to defect. Besides, once we get the drug to go public in a few years he'll be worth tens of millions. I know Parker well enough to know that he wouldn't give up that kind of money. It's why he came to me in the first place."

"Then where is he?" Sheldon growled. "Him not showing like this makes me think he's taking all this a little too lightly."

"He's not," Brooks assured him. "It could be that he's just worn out. I've been pushing him pretty hard to finish up."

"When is the last time you saw him?" Sheldon asked.

"A couple of days ago. Right after I got back from D.C. We met in his lab for about half an hour. He was reviewing the new formula with me again." Brooks smiled. "Gentlemen, he's got it. We are going to own the world in a few years' time."

Still, Sheldon didn't like it. Something just didn't feel right about the whole thing.

Looking over the water reminded him that right now, there was nothing he could do about Parker. And he wasn't going to let it ruin his fishing trip. He set his glass down and stood up. "Come on," he said to Dodson. "Let's go."

CHAPTER THIRTY-TWO

I TURNED my truck off the asphalt and onto a dirt road that snaked through the woods. Brad and I bounced through a dozen ruts and passed up a handful of naturally formed ponds on our way back to the cabin. Finally, it appeared out in front of us, tucked up against the tree like a quiet mecca in the midst of a loud and busy world.

"I know we kinda rushed into all this," Brad said, "but how are going to explain kidnapping Parker? He said he won't say anything, but you know how that goes. He'll get some sleazy lawyer who convinces him to pin as much blame as he can on others."

"Plausible deniability."

"That's it?"

"You have anything better?"

"No," he said, "I guess not."

"Parker doesn't know where he is. There's no way to trace you to it. And no one saw us grab him. He's never seen our faces and no one will see us drop him back off near his house."

"Yeah. Okay."

I parked the truck on the side of a small shed so, in the event that Parker had managed to be looking out a window, he wouldn't see my license plate. We donned our ski masks, walked across the wild grass and onto the front porch. Brad pulled a key out of his pocket and unlocked the front door. We stepped inside.

Brad groaned. "Oh, crap. Well, there's your plausible deniability right there."

"I thought you said you left him tied up."

"I did. But not like that."

Directly in front of us, Wayne Parker was swinging from a low rafter, a bed sheet tied around his neck. His face was blue.

I felt no emotion, no pity for the man. He had been a coward in not standing up to Brooks when he proposed a change in the formula. And he had been a coward by choosing not to face a jury for his crimes.

"I think you need to learn how to tie people up better," I said.

"What are we going to do with him?"

I looked up at him. "I don't know."

"Well, I do," Brad said.

"Does it have anything to do with a swamp filled with alligators?"

"Indeed it does."

CHAPTER THIRTY-THREE

THE CUT through the swamp was somewhat familiar territory now. I rode the skiff up the waterways and cut around a grouping of mangroves before circling around and navigating a stand of cypress. Looking back, I saw an eastern indigo slither across my wake.

I reached the hardwood hammock ten minutes later. I tied off the boat and stepped out, then returned to the same limb I'd sat on a couple days prior. I had a small leather bag slung across my chest. I reached in and took out a can of bug spray. Unless Treadwell had a case of this stuff somewhere, I didn't know how he was making it. I had barely stopped the boat before a cloud of the pesky bloodsuckers were already buzzing around my head. The bats weren't out like they had been the other night when I arrived, and the mosquitoes were bold in their attempts to get at me.

I sprayed my neck and arms and waited for twenty minutes before the scrub rustled to my left and Marcus Treadwell appeared. He was wearing the same jeans and T-shirt as the last time I had seen him. He nodded a greeting and stopped ten feet from me. "Didn't expect to see you again."

"I thought you should know that I've learned who was behind the attack on your troop. Because that's what it was, an attack."

His features seemed to soften a little, though he still maintained a defensive posture. "What do you mean?"

I spread my hands and nodded toward the leather bag. "My phone is in there. I had a conversation the night before last with the scientist who invented the drug that killed your Sergeant Major and your commander. I'd like to take it out and let you listen to it. That okay?"

He nodded his assent.

I withdrew my phone and pulled up the audio file. "You'll hear three voices," I said. "Mine, my partner's, and a Dr. Wayne Parker. I've since verified everything you'll hear him say."

The former Delta operator took a couple of steps forward and listened intently as the conversation with Parker progressed. I watched his face as he moved from curious, to sad, to furious. By the time the recording ended, I could see tears on his cheeks and hatred in his eyes. He finally allowed his legs to buckle and he sat on the ground. It was several minutes before he spoke.

"Did I just hear that a general at the Pentagon and an officer at JSOC did this to my brothers?"

"Yes, Marcus."

"Have they been arrested yet?"

"Not yet. See, the thing is, Dr. Parker… he killed himself earlier today. The guilt of what he had done finally caught up to him. Which is more than I can say for others. He won't be able to testify in court. He had some recordings on his computer, but he didn't have permission to record them and the audio is hazy. So I believe everything he said, and everything I heard. But I don't think it will stand up to a good defense lawyer in court."

"Yeah," Treadwell said thoughtfully. "They're on the golden seat of power. No one can hold them accountable."

"Probably not," I said. "But I didn't come back out to this godforsaken wasteland just to give you an update, Marcus. I came back because you were a warrior. A warrior who was betrayed by men who should have been dedicated to keeping you safe. But instead they used you and your fellow operators as guinea pigs."

"So what are you saying?"

"I want you to come back with me. I think it's time that justice had its day in the sun."

CHAPTER THIRTY-FOUR

"LOOK AT THAT BEAUTY!" The tarpon flopped around on the end of the hook, gleaming on the surface as though it wore a coat of tinfoil. The fish had bony jaws that made it hard to maintain a hook up, and the twenty-minute fight had required a great deal of focus. General Sheldon reeled in more line and successfully brought the tired fish to the side of the boat. "About eighty pounds, don't you think?"

"At least," Ted Dodson said. He leaned over the gunwale and reached out for the fish. Grabbing it, he worked out the hook and, with a final look, released it back into the open water. "Nice one," he said. "That was one hell of a fight."

Sheldon reached back and set a fist on the small of his back. He leaned backward and felt his spine crackle. "That's not as easy as it used to be," he said.

"It could be that you're spending too much time behind a desk these days," Dodson offered.

Sheldon slipped his rod into a holder at the transom and took a seat at the helm where the T-top offered some shade from the striking sun. He reached for his YETI and took a sip of his drink: an ice cold Coca-Cola with some rum added in. He looked over the peaceful water. The water was calm, the fish were hitting, and there wasn't a cloud in the sky. A perfect day, ironically couched in one of the very worst weeks he could remember.

He'd finally gotten rid of Douglas Peterson, and now that pesky investigator, McCleary. But now Parker was missing. Between that and all the cleanup he'd had to arrange by calling in all his favors, it had all become a little more than disconcerting.

Dodson's voice cut across the deck and pulled him from his thoughts. "You ready to get back at it?" Dodson asked.

"I think I'm going to hold off a little longer. Get your line in the water. Hook one and bring him in. I'll help him off it."

In the distance a center console hummed over the water, speeding in their general direction. It swept around them so as not to approach directly and came nearer on a low idle. The driver was a clean-shaven young man wearing the typical garb of a fisherman: long sleeve shirt, wrap-around sunglasses, and a ball cap. Both the shirt and the cap were green and bore matching logos that Sheldon couldn't make out. The young man raised a hand and called out.

"Mind if I approach?"

Ted waved him on.

The young man tossed out his starboard fenders as a courtesy and came in along their port side. "Hope I'm not interrupting, gentlemen."

"Not at all," Ted said and jabbed a thumb toward Sheldon. "He's just trying to decide if he's too old to wrestle in a tarpon. What can we do for you?"

"I'm a representative with Friends of the Keys. They've got me spending the day on the water handing out information on what we do."

"We're just visiting for a couple of days," Ted said. "But what's your pitch?"

"We just want people to know how fragile the wildlife habitats are around here and provide folks with some easy things they can do to help out. With more and more tourists coming down every year, we want people to enjoy their time here and also go home more informed." He grabbed a couple of pamphlets from his back pocket. "Can I leave this with you?"

"Sure," Ted said. "Why not?"

"Great." A branded canvas bag was sitting on the helm seat beside him. "And if you like, I've got some pens I can leave with you. And we got permission to hand out these too." He smiled. "Just so you'll be more likely to remember us." He reached into the bag and brought out a couple of three-ounce liquor bottles. "Either one of you like rum?"

"I sure as hell do," Sheldon boomed. He stood up and stepped to starboard.

The other man eyed them and grinned. "You both are over twenty-one, aren't you? They made me swear I would check everyone's ID, no matter how old they look. But I won't tell if you don't."

"Hand them on over," Sheldon said. "Our lips are sealed." He took the pamphlets, the pens, and the two small bottles of liquor. He took a long look at the latter. "Look at that. You guys have your own label." He looked up and smirked at the young man. "You sure you're into saving the environment and not bootlegging?"

"Absolutely. Listen, I've taken enough of your time. I'm sorry to bother you and I appreciate you listening for a moment. Look us up online when you get some time."

Dodson thanked him and the man brought in the fenders and eased up on the throttle, finally getting back onto plane when he was a hundred yards out. "Nice kid," he said.

"Yeah." Sheldon reached for his YETI, removed the lid, and went over to the ice sitting in the stern. He opened the lid and selected another can of Coke. "Ted, you want in on some of this rum too?"

"You know I do."

He handed over his YETI and Sheldon started to pour.

In the distance, Marcus Treadwell stood at the helm of the center console and sped over the water. He removed his "Friends of the Keys" hat, tossed it on the deck, and rubbed the palm of his hand against the freshly shaven skin of his face.

Today had been a long time in coming. Nearly a year now. So much damage had been done, so much lost. Night after night went by with him seeing the faces of his brothers in his haunted dreams; not a day when he didn't think of Lana and how much he missed being with her.

He couldn't change the past. He couldn't go back and stop evil men from committing evil acts.

But he could avenge his brothers. He could give an eye for an eye. Tooth for tooth. *Life for life.*

He smiled to himself as the wind coasted over him and the motors droned on behind.

By the end of the day, General Benjamin Sheldon and Major Ted Dodson would be dead.

CHAPTER THIRTY-FIVE

IT WAS NEARLY dark by the time the two military officers arrived back at their secluded bungalow a half mile out from Big Torch Key.

They were wiped out. They had discarded their previous plans for the evening, which included grabbing some dinner at The Grumpy Oyster and seeing what they could do to bring a couple of ladies back with them for the night.

Instead of all that, they had arrived back at the bungalow feeling like someone had slipped them a handful of Benadryl. They could hardly keep their eyes open. Sheldon didn't even bother to flip off his loafers before falling onto his bed without even pulling back the covers.

A couple hours ago Ted had made a joke about what exactly was in that rum they had been given. But they both laughed it off and chalked up the sudden exhaustion to the stress of handling all the loose ends over the previous week and Dr. Parker not showing for their meeting in Sarasota.

Dodson's joke was much closer to reality than they could have ever thought.

It was after 1 AM when Sheldon's eyes flicked open and he pushed himself off the bed and stared dumbly out the window. His stomach convulsed and he opened his mouth and vomited all across the floor.

His entire body started to tremble and a sudden heat flared up inside his head. It felt like ants were crawling inside his brain—fire ants. They were multiplying every second and now they felt as though they were burying inside his mind.

He groaned and clapped his hands over his ears. He had to get them out. Flinging open the bedroom door he made his way into the kitchen and grabbed at the side of the counter.

Thunk.

A line of blood started trickling down his forehead.

Thunk.

In his altered state of mind, Sheldon thought it strange that a handgun was sitting on the counter. He hadn't brought one with him. Deep in the back of his mind, the part the ants hadn't gotten to, he recognized it as a Sig Saur P226. It had custom chrome plating and a textured blue polymer grip.

The fire was getting worse, a blazing heat filling the space between his ears. He was past the point of lucidity now. It was too much. The pain. The heat rolling around in his head.

And there it was, the gun, staring at him like a faithful friend.

Thunk.

He grabbed it, and an ingrained, automatic habit caused him to check the load. A round was already in the chamber. Silently thanking whoever had left the gun, he set the end of the barrel to his temple and pulled the trigger.

Ten minutes later, in Ted Dodson's bedroom, another gunshot echoed across the house.

Outside, at the dock, a wary pelican took flight from his perch, and all was quiet.

CHAPTER THIRTY-SIX

John Brooks left the comfort of his office on the top floor of MercoKline's headquarters and took the elevator down to the first floor.

He was nervous. Especially nervous. He had just spent the last five minutes standing in front of the television in his office, watching as CNN's drone zoomed in on the tiny island where, according to the report, the bodies of Major General Benjamin Sheldon and Major Ted Dodson were found. Both men had apparently died by suicide. Each by a single, self-inflicted gunshot wound to the head.

That all sounded a little too familiar.

Brooks had just been with his associates, two days ago on his yacht. There was no way they would have taken their own lives. Not only were they lack enough concern to take such a drastic step, they were both too proud to do such a thing. Especially Sheldon.

Brooks quickly made his way down the hall and gained access to Parker's lab. He went to the corner where the secure refrigerator sat and punched in his code.

Nothing happened.

Frantic, he tried again.

He screamed and slapped the refrigerator repeatedly. He tried the code a final time and, when it still didn't work, he made a quick exit from the lab and took the elevator down to the parking garage.

His Porsche Panamera was parked in the executive section where each morning it was washed and detailed while he was at work. He unlocked his car, opened the door, and got in. He gripped the wheel and took a deep breath, trying to rid himself of the unsettling feeling sitting hard on his chest.

It was the voice behind him that caused him to leave his skin on the seat.

"Hello, John."

* * *

JOHN BROOKS nearly convulsed out of his seat at my friendly greeting. I couldn't help but laugh at the sight of it. His head whipped around to see me sitting behind him wearing a ski mask.

"What do you want?" he cried out.

"You were going somewhere," I said. "Please, continue. Don't let me stop you."

Brooks eyed me suspiciously in the rearview mirror.

"I mean it. Go on."

He hesitated and then turned on the car, put it in gear, and eased out of his space before slowly driving out of the parking garage.

"What do you want?" he asked in a shaky voice.

"John, I think you know why I'm here."

"Oh, God. *Please*. I can give you—"

"Groveling does not become a man. My grandmother told me that on more than one occasion."

"Please, I—"

"Quit groveling. Man, you do not listen very well."

He reached the main road and flipped on his blinker before turning.

"John," I said, "I assume you saw what happened to your friends last night."

He nodded.

"I would hate for that to happen to you. That said, I need you to do something for me. Are you listening?"

"Yes."

"You are going to record a video in which you state your full confession: Parker's research, your intent to twist that research into a new, genetically induced strain of PTSD. You will—"

"How could you know that?" he snapped.

"Have you seen Dr. Parker lately?"

"Oh, God."

"As I was saying, you are also going to name each and every member of the Delta element that you poisoned for monetary gain, and your intent to do it again to our Green Berets. You will describe, in meticulous detail, your business agreement with General Sheldon and Major Dodson, and their roles in this as well, without putting all the guilt on them. You'll take credit for the death of Douglas Peterson and Major William McCleary. When you're done, you'll send that video to every major news station and wait for the police to arrive at your doorstep."

"I—I can't do that."

Another coward.

"Sure you can. You just need the proper motivation. Do you really think I don't have any more of the original formula? Do you really think I was that nearsighted?"

He swallowed hard. "Look—"

"No. *You* look," I growled. "You're going to own what you did. If you miss a single beat, or if I don't like something about your confession, you're going to end up just like your friends."

It was silent in the car for a long while; cars and palms and buildings rolling by.

"Okay," he finally said. "Okay, I'll do it."

"And a couple more things," I added. "You will plead guilty, and if I hear that you reached some kind of plea agreement or hung yourself in prison, I will distribute what you created to your family." His entire body tensed, and before he could threaten me back, I said, "But rest assured that I won't touch them if you do the right thing. Pull over."

I would never harm his family. If I stooped that low, I would be no better than he. But he didn't know my moral limits; he had no idea where I would draw the line.

We were near a public park. He pulled to the curb and I opened my door. "One more thing," I said, "You'll give the police access to the refrigerator in Parker's office. Once you enter the lab with them, the refrigerator will repossess its original settings and your code will work at that time. Try accessing it without them present, and it won't open. You have twelve hours."

"Who are you?"

I slipped out of the car, shut the door, and disappeared into the trees.

CHAPTER THIRTY-SEVEN

I SET the fishing hook on the bottom eyelet and tightened it with another half turn of the reel. I placed the rod in a holder in the gunwale and lowered the fold-down swim patio. The swim patio was a pretty cool feature, but I'd only used it once before, on a dive.

I set my shades aside, peeled off my shirt and tossed it on the back of the helm seat. Then I stepped to the edge of the platform and dove into the water. I swam down, letting the ocean swallow me as I let it wash the events of the last few days off me. There really is nothing like the ocean's salty water to make you whole again. I stopped when the pressure on my ears became too much and took my time getting back to the surface. Once there, I flipped over on my back and closed my eyes against the bright glare of the sun. I bobbed at the surface for a while.

Nothing would bring William McCleary back. Or Douglas Peterson. Or the men Treadwell had lost. But I could rest easy now. The men behind it had gotten their dues.

I stayed in the water for another half hour before getting back on deck. I brought up the swim platform and donned my shirt and sunglasses, then started the engines and gave them some throttle. I rode the boat fast across the water, getting it on plane and feeling the thrilling sensation that can only come from riding over open water.

I worked my way to a dock off the southern end of John Pennekamp State Park and docked the boat. There was a Publix grocery store just across the street. I went inside. There was no line at the customer service desk, and as I stepped up the attending lady smiled at me. "How can I help you?"

I tugged my wallet from my back pocket and plucked out a twenty. I set it on the counter and slid it across. "Two rolls of quarters please."

* * *

I PULLED my boat into a slip behind The Reef. I tied off and cut the engines before stepping out and walking inside. I smiled as I saw a couple of new friends sitting at a table talking with a couple of old friends.

Amy was mixing a drink behind the bar. I bellied up and set the rolls of quarters in front of her.

"What's that?" she asked.

"That is jukebox money. I thought you could keep it somewhere behind the bar. Now when I come in, I don't have to steal from your tips."

"Ryan, I was kidding about the coins. I'm happy to give you a few."

"I know you are. But now you don't have to."

She smiled. "Thanks." She tossed a lime wedge in the drink and then looked back at me. "Oh, I keep meaning to tell you. Ryan, Charlotte is such a gem. I'm so glad she came to stay with me. And I kind of hate that she has to go back to D.C."

"Me too," I said.

You get to know what people are made of when you watch them walk through hell. Charlotte had a heart of gold. She had lost her father and had been nearly killed herself a couple of times, and yet all the while she kept a level head about her. Charlotte was classy, beautiful, and smart, and even though I wasn't ready to move from my wife yet, Charlotte had stirred a small part of me that made me wish I was.

I was going to miss her too.

"She's over there at that table," Amy said. "Go on over and I'll bring you a beer."

"Thanks."

Charlotte was sitting at a table with Brad, Roscoe, and Marcus Treadwell. Marcus looked alive. He was clean shaven now and wearing a contented smile.

"Hey, everyone."

"Ryan," Brad said, "we were just talking about me."

I rolled my eyes and took a seat across from Charlotte, and next to Roscoe, who clapped a hand on my shoulder. "We've missed you around here these last couple days. Everything good?"

"Yeah. It is now."

Charlotte leaned in on her elbows and smiled. "Thanks for everything you did for me." She looked to Marcus. "For both of us."

"I'm glad I could. Marcus, what's your next step?"

"I'm going back to Orlando in the morning. I've got a lot to explain and patch up with Lana. But I hope we can make it work again."

"She's a sweet girl. You take good care of her," I said.

"Promise you'll come see me whenever you're in D.C.," Charlotte said to me. There was a hint of flirtation in her voice.

"I will. I promise."

Amy brought my drink over and we all spent the next hour talking and laughing. There was a sense of new beginnings in the air. I stood up and went to the jukebox, slipped in a quarter, and selected George Strait.

"Darts?" Brad asked.

"Let's do it."

I grabbed the darts out of an old cigar box and handed three red ones to Brad. We backed up to the line and started the game. A couple rounds later I saw someone walk through the door that made me think that I'd drunk five more beers than I actually had.

It was Kathleen.

She was wearing blue jeans, sandals, and a sleeveless blouse. She looked amazing—I still wasn't used to seeing her dressed down.

"I didn't do it," Brad said defensively as she approached.

"I'm sorry to interrupt," she said and took in the room. "Nice place. I can see why you two like it so much. Is there somewhere we can talk?"

"Sure," I said. I took Brad's dart, plucked out the ones we'd already thrown at the board, and returned them to the cigar box. "Right here's as good as any," I said. The place was packed out, even flowing out onto the back deck and the dock.

"What's up?" I asked.

"I want to know, but I don't want to know, about *that*." She tossed her head toward the television above the bar. It was replaying the drone footage from Big Torch Key. The crawler was advertising breaking news about a VP of MercoKline confessing to his complicity in a military cover-up.

Brad shot me a sideward glance, waiting for me to answer.

I looked off into a corner. "Someone told us to make sure that heads rolled."

"Well," she said, "I don't think that person meant for you to go take it literally."

I shrugged. Brad shuffled his feet.

"A hell of a good job, you two. I think I've got the two best agents on the government's payroll."

We started breathing again. "Thanks, Kathleen."

"Yeah," Brad said. "I'll remind you of that next time we screw something up."

There was an old fishnet hanging on the ceiling above Kathleen's head. It started to dance and wobble. I looked up just as something heavy fell from it and flopped onto Kathleen's shoulder.

Kathleen is tough as nails, but her wits were no match for Brad's iguana falling from the sky and landing on her. She screamed—albeit a short, stunted one—and jumped back. The iguana fell off her shoulder, and Brad stepped in and caught it before it hit the floor.

Kathleen cursed and now had the momentary attention of everyone in the place. "What was that thing doing up there?"

Brad frowned. "You know, I'm not sure. Don't be mad at him," he said, petting the reptile.

"I'm not mad at him. I'm mad at *you*."

"Am I still one of the best agents ever?"

"I'm not sure anymore," she said. "But I need a drink."

"I'll get you one," he said, and started toward the bar.

Kathleen smiled. "I love you, Brad."

"I love you too, Kathleen."

"I was talking to the iguana."

Brad stopped and sighed, then looked toward his pet. "I think you're getting a name change, bud."

GET READY FOR SAVAGE STORM

A ROGUE FEDERAL AGENT

A PUZZLING MISSION

And a twist he never saw coming...

When a federal agent goes offline, Ryan Savage is pulled off a training exercise and sent to undercover the truth behind the agent's chain of mysterious choices.

Ryan is sent to Cuba, where his search for the elusive agent lands him in a tangled web of deceit, behind which lies a horrific secret.

And as the truth comes to light, he begins to rethink everything he was told about his mission and where his allegiances should lie.

A storm is headed straight for the Florida Keys... and into Ryan Savage's life.

AUTHOR'S NOTE

Thank you for reading *Savage Justice*! I hope you enjoyed stepping out of your world and into Ryan's for a little while.

It's been a lot of fun writing these books; getting Savage into trouble and then finding ways to get him out of it.

If you enjoyed the book, please consider reviewing it on the book's Amazon sales page. It can be as brief as you'd like, and it can help more than you know.

STAY UP TO SPEED

To be notified of upcoming releases as soon as they come out, sign up at http://bit.ly/2pESrFX.

Follow Jack on Facebook: fb.me/jackhardinauthor

Say hello: jack.w.hardin00@gmail.com

57365626R00132